Nurse Kit Carson's Knife & Gun Club

The first five episodes…

L.S.Collison

ISBN: 978-1-7322290-8-2

Artwork "Requiem" Oil on wood by Gregory Block

CONTENTS

ACKNOWLEDGMENTS

To all the caregivers in the trenches of healthcare, thanks for showing up. It will be duly noted on your record.

ONE

FRIDAY NIGHT KNIFE & GUN CLUB

Friday night
Kit Carson, RN

Ten twenty-five P.M. It's snowing like hell, defroster turned up as high as she'll go, ice on the wiper blades, I can't see for shit. It's another Friday night, my weekend to work, and they're predicting the blizzard of the century. You'd think people would stay home on a night like this but everybody and their brother is out, stocking up on necessities—donuts, diapers, toilet paper, beer—in case they're snowed in tomorrow. I've got me a tank; this baby'll get through anything. Burns gas but she's reliable. I mean, you've got to get to work, right? Kids are at home, alone, but I keep an eye on them with my iCam app. They've got their phones, they've got their games, they've got each other. They'll be alright.

Wyatt's in charge, there's a Glock-17 under the bed and believe-you-me he knows how to use it. Calamity doesn't have the hand strength yet to load a gun and release the safety, nor is she mature enough to be trusted with one. But she insists on sleeping with her own weapon—a butcher knife—under her pillow in case her big brother is sleeping when they break in. Even at her age she knows a knife can be every bit as deadly as a firearm. And in case all hell breaks loose, in case the war starts when I'm not home, old man Henderson lives next door. I see the light from his television as I'm leaving for work. Henderson's got an arsenal in his house. He's prepared for the Second Coming, a meth addict, or a G-man who might come knocking at his door to take away his inalienable rights. This is the wild, Wild West baby, you better believe it.

The snowplows are out in force. Chink, chink, chink, sounds like jingle bells but Christmas is over, except for the bills. The wind's come up, the snow is already drifting across the pavement the plow just cleared. I'm glad I've got four-wheel drive and big ass tires on this bitch.

Now I'm pulling up to my place of employment, High Plains Trauma and Medical Center, I see two ambulances parked on the Emergency ramp, and one pulling away. Nights like this are always the worst, you'd think people would just find someplace warm, curl up and go to sleep. I sure as hell would, if I didn't have to work. Bears hibernate, why can't we? Looks like the visitor parking lot is completely full which means we'll have families camping out in the halls, kids crying, cell phones ringing, coffee pot on all night long. The Emergency Department is the main portal to the Inferno, and there are more circles of hell in this dark tower than Dante ever dreamed of. But don't let my morbid sense of humor, stained by the blood and guts of my profession fool you. Deep inside my pink heart weeps.

Park my four wheeled beast in the lot reserved for **Attending Physicians Only**. Won't be any of them in here on a night like this. It'll be house staff in the trenches with us tonight. At least we've got a good group of yearlings who know enough to listen to us. And a really sharp second-year surgical resident. Confident but not cocky. She knows her shit, she's on the ball, she can take the heat.

Getting out of my car now, I'm always aware of my surroundings. Lock up, lights flash, beep-beep. Keys in my pocket, I touch the butt of my Smith and Wesson swinging at my right hip. For reassurance. Walking through the parking garage can be one of the most dangerous parts of the shift. Even with ten security guards on duty—it's a big medical center—they center they can't be everywhere at once. My new holster matches my Kevlar, I ordered them online from my favorite nursing supply store, Scrubs and More. So stylish and comfortable; the vest even has a pocket to carry extra clips.

"Cause I wanna be a cowboy, baby." I'm singing that old Kid Rock song, my stethoscope looped around my neck like an urban cowboy's bolo tie. I'm wearing my new boots, cute white cowboy boots with arch support and memory foam insteps—great for riding in the saddle or running the hospital halls. Got them from Scrubs and More too. Boots and guns, it's a western thing, part of our culture. Who we are. Our little TICU victory rap we do when we discharge a patient to go to some lesser level of care—goes like this:

We're Trauma nurses, don't fuck with us
Bad ass, uh-huh! That's us, oh, yeah!
We can save your life or we can burn you down
Bad ass, uh-huh! That's us, oh yeah!

(There's a little booty shake that goes with that, and a thing we do with our hands.)

*

I've been working at the hospital for eight years now; the last four in TICU – Trauma Intensive Care Unit. Haven't been able to get off the night shift yet, but I'm glad to have a job. It's tough these days with all the cutbacks and cost-containment measures. The bottom line of my check register is dangerously close to being in the red—and I've got four more days until payday—but I'll make it. I'm tough. I can make it on my own.

Stamping snow off my boots like I'm doing some kind of country western line dance, I'm coming through the staff door with a handful of other stragglers all bundled up in winter survival gear. We night shifters all have that haggard, sleep-starved look on our faces. There was talk awhile back of implementing a retinal scan for identification, but it was too costly. We still scan our badges against the barcode reader, just like the old days. It's kind of like airport security—a worthless procedure but I guess it makes people feel safe. There are so many ways for Killer Joe to get inside this complex – I mean, a hospital is a public building, right?

And with so many employees, who's to say one of us isn't crazy? Our pharmacy has been robbed twice in the past year, at gunpoint. Both were inside jobs. One of the thieves, a maintenance worker, didn't want narcotics; she wanted anti-rejection meds for her brother who lost his job – and his medical insurance – six months after his transplant. He couldn't afford the medication, rejected the kidney she had given him and had to go back on dialysis. Which, ironically, the government pays for—even though it's far more expensive and way less effective than a transplant. When people are desperate, there's no telling what they'll do.

Walking down the hall, breathing in that good old hospital smell, that mixture of antiseptic, cafeteria food and humanity. Those of us just coming on duty are waiting for the elevators, the snow from our boots and coats melting into little puddles. We don't all know each other but we know we're part of the pack. We share comments about the road conditions, the weather forecast, the upcoming Super Bowl as we're waiting for the steel box which seems to be stopping at every single floor.

Ding! The elevator finally lands, empties its load and we crowd in, like holocaust victims. Somebody presses the button and the doors close. We all call out our floor numbers and the self-appointed operator pushes the buttons. The numbers of the floors light up and the steel cage rattles and squeaks, stopping on the second floor to let off one nurse and pick up two lab techs. We're all dressed pretty much the same, in worker's uniforms; proletariat scrub suits of various colors and patterns. Some wear white lab coats over top of scrubs. Those are usually the house staff, the baby docs. The lab techs wear white coats too, but you always know the lab techs because they carry Easter baskets—plastic caddies filled with goodies like needles, syringes and little glass tubes with colorful tops, lavender, red and blue. But Easter is a long way off.

We all squeeze in a little tighter to make room for the new arrivals. The doors close, we go up, but not very quickly—and with a lot of creaking and groaning. I imagine a bunch of miners in the basement toiling away with shovels and picks. They've harnessed a little burro to a capstan; he's plodding round and round and round, hauling the elevator up like a cart of rocks. Those miners don't know if it's day or night down there in the bowels of the earth but I'll bet they're getting tired, and that poor little burro too. They all just want to go home.

Sometimes I wish I had the miner's job instead of the nurse's job. Surely there wouldn't be as much documentation to drudge over. I wouldn't have to worry about accidentally offing anybody by pushing the wrong drug, or misinterpreting a heart monitor, or fucking up a cardiac output measurement.

It never ceases to amaze me, the power of life and death in my hands. Anyone can make a mistake, especially late at night if you didn't get enough sleep that day and you've got other things on your mind. Maybe that's why I drink too much coffee and carry a few extra pounds. I need that caffeine and sugar rush to keep me awake. I've started smoking again, just to keep me alert. I'm a good nurse, I know I am, but no one is perfect and life is so unpredictable. You can't possibly prepare for everything, can you? Just do your damn best, that's all you can do. I get off on the fifth floor and turn left. Above the double doors, **Trauma Intensive Care**. A small sign next to the door says **All visitors please check in with the receptionist and take a seat in the waiting room**. But on night shift there is no receptionist, are you kidding me? We nurses decide who gets to enter the hallowed gates. At night we call all the shots.

Stepping inside I hear the sighs of the ventilators. Oooh paah, ooh paah. I hear the beeping of a disgruntled intravenous pump and the whining electric motor of the portable x-ray machine as Duke, the rad-tech, pushes it down the hall. Over-laid on the background of electronic sounds is the bright chatter of human voices. It's a busy unit, Trauma Intensive Care. People coming and going at all hours, excitement in the air like the smell of popcorn. It's kind of like a carnival, a three-ring circus, a Wild West show complete with Buffalo Bill and Annie Oakley. We're usually oversold and you're guaranteed to see amazing feats of life-saving derring-do and some fancy roping to boot. Maybe even a miracle or two.

Intensive Care Units are always brightly lit; we are the land of the midnight sun. Studies have shown the ill effects of continuous light on the body's circadian rhythm; it jacks with the pineal gland, it leads to disorientation, confusion, and slower healing times. People need darkness, we need rest. We need to dream. But this is no country for old men – or old nurses. Sleep must wait. If you're in Intensive Care, it's because your life is on the edge and you are dangling by a thread. Your vital signs, your heart rhythm, your arterial pressures, your pulmonary pressures, your intracranial pressures – we make them our business. Here, there is no privacy. We watch you closely; we invade your every drug-induced dream. But we keep you alive. And if you're well enough to complain, you're ready for discharge, you're outta here, sucker.

Coat and backpack in the locker, now I'm sitting in the conference room trying to warm my hands, holding a cup of bitter black sludge that passes for coffee. Listening to a taped report by the off-going shift along with my co-workers: Tim, Marty, Chris, Melanie, Jeff, Morgan, Russell, Jane, Cid. We've got a good posse on tonight. As nurses we all depend on one another, we work as a team. We've each got our own patients but we watch each other's back, we keep an eye out for all the patients on the unit. And we've got to be ready to respond to a code.

There are different codes for various emergencies. If a fire breaks out you call the operator and the operator pages "Mr. Gallagher"—our code word for fire. Imagine the pandemonium if the operator used the F word!

If a patient crashes—if their heart stops or they go into V-fib—you push the magic red button. Doing that alerts the operator to announce, "COR ZERO," along with the floor and the room number. When you press the magic red button you're calling the Mission Impossible team to come help you. You're calling the resident docs, the interns, the nursing supervisor. You're calling nurses who are expert in starting IV lines, respiratory therapists who can set up a ventilator and intubate, if the doc can't. You're summoning lab techs and runners. It's like giving a big party and having all your best friends show up—a little out of breath, gifts in hand, expectant looks on their faces.

*

The unit's got sixteen patients tonight and a trauma case still in surgery; a self-inflicted gunshot wound. Somebody who shouldn't have access to a weapon, it happens all the time. She'll come to our unit as soon as they're finished, if she doesn't die on the table. Tim Rhodes is the TCIU charge nurse; we all call him Tonto. Tonto's an old hippie, he doesn't carry a gun. He don't go heels, as they used to say in the wild west days. He wears moccasins and keeps his hair in a long gray braid down his back. Claims to have some Ute blood, or maybe it's Arapaho, I can't remember. Calls himself a shaman. Tonto has studied the healing ways of his people, he burns sage and sings Indian prayers, but he also knows the high-tech side of twenty-first century western medicine and critical care nursing. He's boss, alright. They say he's bad-ass with a bow and arrow and by the looks of his pectorals filling out the lose cotton sleeves of his scrubs, I don't doubt it at all.

Tonto gives us our assignments then we all make rounds together with the off-going shift. I've got Mr. Sobee for like, the fifth night in a row. Coriolanus Sobee, a 43-year-old white male with multiple trauma, is what we call in this business, a train wreck. Meaning he's a real mess, every system in his body is jacked up. Actually, he was in a wreck of sorts. Motorcycle meets bus; bus wins. Bus always wins. Sobee's got a season ticket; he's been in ICU nearly two weeks and isn't going anywhere anytime soon. His life is on hold. He's ventilator dependent, on multiple antibiotics, in traction, and in an artificially induced coma to keep his intracranial pressures down. Miranda, his wife, went home earlier today. Exhausted. I hope she gets a good night's sleep because her husband isn't out of the woods yet. It's going to be a long haul.

I do an initial head-to-toe assessment on Mr. Sobee. Daisy, the off-going nurse, put on his tunes. Music is playing softly, Mozart, I think it is. Sobee's wife says he loves classical music and requests we play it as much as possible. A Mozart-loving Harley rider, that's kind of odd, isn't it? But then again, maybe not. Why do I presume to know what sort of music a Harley rider would prefer? Maybe he writes poetry too, who knows? Maybe he likes to knit socks. I have noticed that when the classical music is on his heart rate drops to the seventies, his oxygen saturation improves, his blood pressure stabilizes. Is there a healing quality inherent in such elite music, or is it soothing simply because Mr. Sobee is familiar with it? Or is it just random chance? I should make a study, write it up for *American Journal of Nursing*. Yeah, right. Like I've got the time.

My other patient is Shanna Jackson, a sixteen-year-old gunshot victim. Poor kid got caught in the crossfire of a neighborhood shoot-out. Sure, she had a gun in her handbag, but she wasn't really expecting anything. Just walking home from school with her girlfriend, they were probably laughing about something silly like teenagers do, when—bipbipbip—she's lying on the sidewalk, a bullet through her chin, another through her right arm, taking half her right breast with it, a rather messy mastectomy. Her quick-thinking bestie called nine-eleven on her cellphone and stayed with her, using her mittened hand to stop the blood pumping out of Shanna's brachial artery. Now that's what I call a BFF, that's who I want by my side when the shooting starts.

Shanna's condition is stable; she'll probably go to the floor tomorrow, if all goes well tonight. And home in another couple of days. Back to school in a week or two. She's one of the lucky ones. Her mother's sitting in a plastic chair next to her, beside the IV pole. Her head's resting on Shanna's bed, she's snoring. Usually we don't allow family to spend the night in the room, not in TICU, but sometimes we make exceptions. Like tonight. It's my call, I could boot her out if I thought it was best. But I let her stay.

Shanna opens her eyes and gives me that look. That look that says, please don't hurt me!

"Hi, I'm Kit, I'm your night nurse." I'm touching her right wrist below the dressing, feeling for pulses distal to her injury. "Just checking your vital signs, your dressings, your IV and all that. You're in the intensive care unit." I give her a confident smile.

At the sound of my voice her mother sits up and takes hold of her daughter's left hand.

"It's alright, baby, your mama's here, your mama's here. You're gonna be alright, honey."

I glance at Shanna's monitor screen, reading all the information it provides. I make note of her intravenous solution; what it is, how fast it's running. I examine the needle insertion site to make sure it's patent and not infiltrating. I check her urine collection bag and note the quantity and color. Observation is a big part of my job.

"Are you having any pain, Shanna? Don't try and talk, your jaw is wired. Just raise your left hand if you're hurting."

She pulls her left hand from her mother's and raises it like an eager school child, a teacher's pet. The mother's eyes fly to mine. "Can't you give her something, nurse? She's hurting real bad."

Nod my head. Pain relief is another big part of my job. Ask and you shall receive.

"What number is your pain, Shanna? On a scale of zero to ten. With zero being no pain at all and ten being the worst pain you have ever experienced." I reach for the communication board on her bedside table and hold it so she can see it. It's a dry erase board with a blue marker tied to it. At the top there's a pain scale with numbers and cartoon faces making various expressions ranging from pleasure to agony. She points to the number 8, and a grimacing face.

"I'll give you some pain reliever in your IV line and set you up with a self-administration pump. We'll get you taken care of, don't you worry, I'm here to help."

She takes the board and manages to write *Angel of Mercy* in wobbly letters on the communication board. I'm not sure if she means me, or if she's religious and is invoking the heavenly hosts, or maybe it's her mother she's referring to. But a dose of morphine and a pump and she'll think she's in heaven. Wish I could give the mother something to help her sleep, because this place sure ain't the Holiday Inn.

Cid's patient is the one we've got to worry about tonight. Hart Anderson is a twenty-eight-year-old man who got run over by his own car this afternoon. It's a strange story, but then they all are. Every time you hear the back story you think, that was dumb. I wouldn't have done that. But the truth is we all do dumb things everyday but somehow get away with them.

Mr. Anderson was in his two-car garage this afternoon, jump-starting the dead battery in his pick-up truck, his eight-year-old kid in the cab. The kid accidentally put the truck in gear, the emergency brake didn't hold or wasn't on, and the truck crushed Dad against the wall. Quick-thinking kid calls nine-eleven first, then his mother. Anderson was flown in from Goodland, Kansas, not long before the snow started flying and all the choppers were grounded. Got out of OR at change-of-shift after six hours on the table; status post-surgical repair of his entire thorax, sounds like. Why the hell he wasn't DOA is anybody's guess; maybe his angel of mercy had a say in that. Anyway, his wife and kid and a neighbor, they drove here from Goodland through the snow storm. They're all camped out in the waiting room with the families of other patients; it's a regular Boy Scout Jamboree.

As soon as she's sure Mr. Anderson is stable and presentable Cid sends for his family. She lets them come to the bedside for a few minutes, then hustles them back to the waiting room and tucks them in with Styrofoam cups of instant hot chocolate. "Try to get a little shut-eye," she says. "I'll come get you if anything changes."

Cid is an amazing nurse. She's Wonder Woman in red white and blue scrubs. Her good nature, her upbeat attitude, it rubs off on all of us. If I ever end up in TICU, I hope Tonto assigns Cid to take care of me. She's my idol; I wish I had her life. A great husband, two blonde boys with straight teeth and a third kid on the way. It's a girl, due in May. Perfect all-American family. Except John works days, they hardly see each other, but at least there's always one parent home with the kids. They tag team it, giving high fives as they pass through the door. Date night, once a month on Cid's weekend off. I feel a little jealous 'cause I want her life. I want somebody on my team.

*

It's just after one A.M. and Tonto has a fresh pot of coffee brewing in the lounge. When he makes the coffee it always smells a little like burning sage and I swear I can feel my spirit being cleansed. So far Cid's patient is hanging in there. I got Shanna's pain under control, called the resident to get an order for a PCA pump – why the hell she didn't come out of OR with one is beyond me. Anyway, she's sleeping now, and everything looks good. Mama's sleeping too, sitting in the chair, her drooling face on Shanna's bed just like I found her when I first came in the room. I drape a warm blanket across her back, it's the least I can do. Hang Shanna's midnight antibiotics, check her dressings, her wound drains, measure her urine output, check it for blood. Everything looks good—for now. Wash my hands and go next door to spend some time with Mr. Sobee. Outside the snow is coming down sideways, the wind sings a lullaby and I wish I could curl up on the bed beside him.

Cid asks me to keep an eye on her patients while she goes to the nurses' lounge (funny word, because when do we get to lounge?) to phone home.

"I texted John to let him know I made it in alright but he likes to hear my voice. He always likes to say goodnight." She smiles and I feel a rush of envy.

Later on, Cid returns the favor. My work is caught up and my patients are stable so I'm going to take a short break. I'm going to go down and get a snack from the machines then stop by the ED to see if Dillon is working tonight. Dillon and I used to date, way back when. We're still friends. We still get together every so often, for old time's sake. I don't know what happened, there was just something missing, maybe it was me.

The cafeteria is closed at night. We're told it costs too much to keep it open twenty-four seven. Apparently the night shift doesn't need hot food. We're a breed who exists on leftover pizza, Doritos, Chinese take-out, candy bars, whatever. Here's proof. I feed two dollars into the machine, push the button and wait for my Twinkies to drop down. Eat them both standing up, one right after the other. Mmmmm, love that airy texture of the golden sponge cake, that creamy filling caressing my tongue. A cup of caffeine to chase it, maybe a quick cigarette and I'll be good to go the rest of the night.

Walking down the hall, I check on the kids using the iCam app on my phone. Both of them are zonked out. They're in Wyatt's room; they sleep together when I'm not home. Calamity's afraid to sleep in her own bed. She still sleeps with me on nights I'm home. Maybe I'll be able to get off night shift one of these days, and have a normal life.

Down on the ground floor the Emergency Department is ripping, they are in full combat mode, it's the Friday Night Knife and

Gun Club with the usual shootings and stabbings, mostly between family members and friends, or drug deals gone bad. You'd think people could just get along, it's so much easier. But I know it's not that easy. I once had a gun, my own gun, held to my head by a man who said he loved me more than life itself. My ex. Lucky me, the cops came with superior weaponry and somehow I still have a head. Somehow, they talked him down. I didn't become a statistic, one of those family murder-suicides that everybody just shakes their heads over. Maybe my angel of mercy was on duty that day. But let's not go there; tonight is not the night to think about that.

The shelters must all be full tonight. They're working up a couple of homeless people with chest pain brought in by ambulance. Chest pain always buys you a few hours out of the cold on a hospital gurney—which is a hell of a lot more comfortable than a cardboard box in two feet of snow. And there's the usual assortment of abdominal pains, psychiatric cases, colicky babies, and gomes from the home—that's our code word for nursing home patients. The waiting room is overflowing with walk-ins, it's like an Irish wake in there, only there are more Mexicans than Irish in this town.

Dillon gives me the overview; we're having a cup of coffee in the ED lounge, a dreary, windowless cubby hole that smells like a wet dog on a night like this.

"How's your shift going, Babe?" He still calls me that, it's vaguely irritating. Before I can answer his cell phone rings, he's listening. "Shit, two ambulances five minutes out, they're bringing us a whole family with CO poisoning."

"'Tis the season."

"Sorry, I gotta go." Dillon slams his coffee and starts for the door. "Hey Babe, wanna do breakfast in the morning?"

"I can't. The kids."

"Still haven't found a night sitter?"

I shake my head.

"Too bad. Hey, call me sometime. When you're free."

"Yeah, right. Maybe when Calamity turns eighteen?" I look at my watch, I've already been gone fifteen minutes. I check my patients' heart rhythms using the app on my phone. Looking good, but I need get back upstairs, I've got to give two units of blood to Shanna, run a cardiac index on Sobee, and catch up on charting. Dillon is already gone, he's getting ready for the new arrivals, he's notifying the hyperbaric team. Time for a two-minute nicotine break, then back to work. My coat is up in my locker, I borrow Dillon's, he left it draped over the back of the chair.

Stand outside on the ramp with a few other smokers, we're huddled around the butt can like hobos around a campfire. Technically, we're not supposed to smoke on the ambulance ramp but it's late at night, who cares? Nobody says much, we're just filling our lungs as fast as we can, we're stamping our feet to keep our toes from freezing. A gust of wind whips around the corner pelting us with crystals of stinging snow and we instinctively turn our backs to it, like cattle in a snowstorm, sheltering our cancer sticks. My God it's cold but the nicotine rush is worth it. Oh, here come the ambulances with the carbon monoxide victims, their blinking lights like lassos twirling. I inhale one last hit before going back inside.

Walking down the hall I pass Paul, one of the technicians, rolling a supply of portable oxygen tanks to the Emergency Department. At night the techs are runners, they go all over the hospital, to Central Supply, to the Laundry, to the morgue. In the old days Paul was an orderly, but there are no more orderlies, there are no more aides; there are patient care assistants and medical technicians. They're still paid shit but they have better titles. Nobody complains. These days we're all glad to have a job.

"Hey Paul, how's it going?" He looks like a heart attack waiting to happen. Overweight, but I don't know how—he must walk thirty miles a night just doing his job. Probably eats too much supersize with fries. Well, when you make beans and you have no chance of ever making much more than a hill of beans, the only pleasure you can afford is the feel-good rush that comes from a huge carb load, that secret sauce and those greasy, salty fries. Plop your fat ass on the couch after work, turn on cable TV and get fucked up on a six-pack of cheap beer. Because you'll never be able to save enough to make a difference, so might as well go down numb.

"It's going, it's going," Paul says. Just like he says every night. "Just not going fast enough." He laughs at his sad little joke. Just like he does every night.

*

I'm waiting for the elevator to take me back up to the TICU when the call comes over the hospital intercom: **"Dr. Dillinger, Newborn Nursery. Dr. Dillinger, Newborn Nursery. Dr. Dillinger, Newborn Nursery."**

It's a joke, right? That's my first thought. I think of all the little babies wrapped in receiving blankets nestled in their mothers' arms. But the blue alarm lights are flashing and my blood freezes cold. Dr. Dillinger is our code word for a shooter on the loose. We have been preparing for this for months and even though we have a bunch of armed guards all over the hospital, shooters will always have the advantage of surprise. We have a metal detector, sure, but not at every door. There are so many ways to get into and out of this hospital, the Emergency Department being the most straightforward—but a shooter in Newborn Nursery? What kind of sicko would do that?

I know the drill. We are to report to battle stations immediately; we're on automatic lockdown. This is the Alamo, this is Desert Storm, this is World War Three. This is why I carry a gun—to protect myself and my patients—this is my duty. But if I had my car keys in my pocket instead of upstairs in my locker, I know where I would be heading right now. My kids need me too. If I had my keys on me, I would be out the fire exit, I would be gone. But I don't so I will do my duty.

The elevators are inoperable; I have to go up five flights of stairs. Drawing my firearm, I run down the hall to the stairwell, put my ear against the door to listen for footsteps coming down. All quiet. With a burst of adrenalin I pull open the door and lunge in, my piece held straight out in front of me. Just like on TV, I make a sweep with my eyes and my gun. Seeing nothing – nobody – I bound up the stairs two at a time, my heart is a jackhammer. On the third floor landing I have to stop for breath, I can't catch my breath. But third floor is Newborn Nursery, that's where the shooter is. Look! The door's opening! Oh shit! Point the gun, my finger on the trigger but the gun is shaking and I'm peeing my pants, I feel the warm rush of liquid down both legs. There he is—squeeze the trigger—kill that son-of-a-bitch!

Oh my God, it's Colt Rankin, one of the L & D interns. I would have shot him, I would have killed him dead—except I forgot to release the safety. Thank you sweet Jesus! What a blazing idiot, I would have been a murderer. Now he sees me – oh no! He's going for his piece, he's—

"Don't shoot! Dr. Rankin, don't shoot me. I'm a nurse, I'm Kit, from TICU! I'm a nurse!"

He leans against the door. "Sweet Jesus."

"What happened? What's going on?"

Rankin's a mess, he's shaking, he can't seem to find the words. He retches but nothing comes out, just a little stream of bile. "Dr. Rankin, are you OK? Are there casualties?"

His eyes are vacant holes. "They're – God." He gasps and gags again, like a cat trying to rid itself of a hairball. "They're all – it's." I see spatters of blood on his lab coat and somehow I know they aren't from delivering a baby. His hands are bloody, he's got blood on his glasses and in his hair.

"Look, Dr. Rankin, I have to get to my station, to TICU. Stay here 'til the cops come. Guard the door!" I leave him there, huddled in the corner. I hope he's not hurt, I didn't even stop to check. I put my pistol back in the holster and call nine-eleven on my cell phone, but dispatch says they've already got the call a hundred times over. They're on it, take cover. Help is on the way.

I pocket my cell phone and bound up the stairs. At the door to the fourth floor I stop again, put my ear against it and listen carefully. On the other side I hear voices shouting, I hear crying. But I've got to get to my post.

The operator's voice, pinched and tight, comes over the loudspeaker. Dr. Dillinger, Labor and Delivery. Dr. Dillinger, Labor and Delivery. Dr. Dil – "The Operator's voice sounds like glass breaking. Who—where—is this monster? L and D now? Are there more than one? Gunshots from above—bipbipbipbip. Somebody's coming down the steps, they're above me. Heavy footsteps. I'm shaking, I'm shaking, pistol in hand, I'm crouching down, I am trying not to lose it. Footsteps louder, the jingling of keys. It's a cop—no—it's one of our security guards. Or is it somebody dressed in a security guard's uniform? How do I know this isn't the killer?

"Stop! Hands in the air!" I yell, letting out a big fart, it sounds like a gun shot.

The man in the guard uniform stops and looks up, sees me with the bead on him. "I'm a nurse, TCIU! Who the fuck are you?"

"I'm a Security Guard! Put that damn thing down before you kill me." He comes up to the landing next to me, huffing and puffing. "Just take cover, OK? We don't need any more shootings. We don't need any more dead. My partner's dead, he's dead, and I'm trying to secure the floor, somebody's shot out the monitors."

"What's going on?"

"Some psycho, an ex-boyfriend of one of the nurses. Marta. She called dispatch just before he blew her away. She had time to give us his name. Said he used to work here. They're running a background check on him." The guard is still trying to catch his breath. Beneath the bill of his hat, his forehead is dotted with sweat. "So we've got to assume he knows the hospital, he knows every door, every linen closet, every hiding place there is."

"What's he want?"

"What do any of them want? A first class ticket to hell. This nutter must've brought in his whole armory. He's shooting up babies and mothers and nurses, he's making his way through the hospital, and the collateral damage is bad – employees are shooting each other, stray bullets killing family members. I'd advise you to hide yourself until the SWAT team gets here."

"I can't. I've got to protect my patients. What's this guy look like?"

"That's the problem. He's wearing a lab coat. He looks like any one of you-all. He used to be one of you-all." He says that like he thinks we all have the potential to turn into monsters.

"Don't shoot Dr. Rankin, he's down there on the third floor landing." Leaving the guard in the stair well, I open the fifth floor door and run down the hallway that leads to TICU, my gun drawn. Run past the waiting room, where the lights are off but the television set is on and kids are crying. I burst through the double doors, ready to fire, but where is everybody?

Zip – blat! A bullet rushes past my head, strikes the wall behind me. Who's shooting? Is it friendly fire? One of my co-workers? Or is it the killer? I duck into Sobee's room and take cover behind the ventilator. Ooh pah, ooh pah, the machine breathes away sounding like Darth Vader. Mozart is still playing on the stereo, a woodwind concerto, music from another century. Just stay calm, I tell myself. Then somebody's alarm go off, it's a heart rate alarm, but it's not my patient, it's Cid's patient, it's Mr. Anderson. My phone app shows me his monitor. He's tachycardic, heart rate of 182, which is what mine feels like right now. Another round of shots, and I hear an explosion, like a bullet hit a ventilator or an oxygen pipe in the wall. Looking out the glass doors I see the surgical resident crouching behind the COR cart, she's got her gun drawn, she's ready.

Oh God, it's him, he's here, he's in TICU! Shots sound like popcorn in the microwave. But Cid's patient is in trouble, he needs help, where the fuck is Cid? And what am I doing? Am I a nurse or a vigilante? I should go to Mr. Anderson's room, I should back up Cid, her patient needs me. But my legs are numb, my gun is suddenly too heavy to lift, it's like I'm frozen. I've spent all my adrenalin, all that's left is fear. My pants are wet and all I can do is peek out from behind the ventilator. It's all I can do, just to watch. I want to cover my head, close my eyes and listen to Mozart, still playing. A beautiful concerto from another century playing in the middle of madness, it's like a time warp.

He's standing in front of this room, Mr. Sobee's room, he's looking in. A little man, not big at all, not like I imagined. He's dressed in surgical scrubs, complete with mask and booties, he's wearing a white lab coat. In his hands, a reliable old AK-47. A common household weapon. Who would have thought? Something startles him. He spins around and empties a clip into the nurses' station. I can't see who he's firing at—I can't see if anybody's hit—but I see Tonto coming up behind him. Tonto's unarmed but he's got a high velocity foam fire extinguisher. He cracks the shooter on the back of the head, dropping him to his knees with a grunt. The weapon falls out of his hands and Shanna's mother comes running out of the room to grab it.

But the killer isn't finished, no sir. He's come prepared. Plenty more where that came from and he's going down in a blaze of rage. Now he's reaching for a something under his lab coat, a handgun. Tonto sees him, he's quick. He pulls the pin of the fire extinguisher and blasts him in the face with a stream of potassium acetate, covering him from head to toe with white foam. Blinded, howling, the shooter gropes under his lab coat and pulls out a pistol—a Glock 17—but before he can blow anybody away Tonto jumps on top of him, pins him to the floor. With a blood-curdling war cry he jams a needle into his jugular vein and drives the plunger home. I don't know what was in that syringe but the shooter is twitching like he's dangling from the end of the rope, his eyes blood red, he's in a full tonic-clonic seizure; snorting, foaming at the mouth and looking like the devil himself. And then he collapses, he's limp on the floor. Unconscious. Or maybe he's dead, I don't know.

"Got you, you crazy sick bastard," says Tonto, tying the man's hands behind his back with a roll of surgical tape. He hobbles his ankles too, like a roped calf at the Western Stock Show.

One by one we come creeping out from our hiding places to stare at the carnage. Tonto's talking on his cell phone, his voice is calm, like he's ordering a pizza. He's talking to the police, giving his location, and when he's finished he puts it in his pocket. He starts doing his Native American prayer dance, wailing in some ancient language as he hops on one foot then the other in his beaded deerskin moccasins.

Something's burning, it's not sage, it smells like an electrical fire. Somebody's pulled the red handle, the overhead sprinklers are raining down, white lights are flashing, an alarm sounds.

Another alarm sounds, the cardiac monitor alarm. It's Cid's patient, Mr. Anderson, he's flat-lined, he's in full cardiac arrest. I dash to his room, slip sliding on blood, water and foam and I mash on the magic red button, wondering if anybody will respond to the code. Grab the paddles, charge the defibrillator, I'm ready to deliver the shock.

But my coworkers are out in the nurses' station, they're gathered around Cid. Our very own Wonder Woman is lying face down in a pool of blood. Her stethoscope is still wrapped around her neck, her pistol still clenched in her hand.

Tonto is still dancing, his arms raised to the sky. High above the cry of alarms and the wail of sirens I hear his voice, a coyote's thin howl.

***

Two

SATURDAY NIGHT KNIFE & GUN CLUB

Saturday night
Kit Carson, RN
In my dream the bad guy was trying to kill me. I couldn't make out his face, but I knew he was the bad guy because of his black hat. In my dream, I drew my gun, but it came out of the holster reluctantly. I was moving sooo slooooow. I took aim just below the black hat. Now the bad guy's face was materializing out of the shadows, it was coming into focus, illuminated by a golden light from above. I squeezed the trigger. In my dream the face became Wyatt's. He looked at me sorrowfully in that last instant before the bullet found its mark.

*

I awoke in a cold sweat. Wyatt, shaking my shoulder impatiently, Calamity's plaintive voice whining like a gnat in my ear.

"Mommy, wake up, pleeeease? We're hungry. There's nothing left to eat."

I buried my head under the pillow and mumbled, "Grab some money out of my saddle bags. Go buy Pop Tarts or something."

"Mom," Wyatt said in a stern and strangely adult voice. "Wake up. The money's all gone."

Get a grip, my conscience chided in agreement. *You're out of work, out of money –you're in deep shit, woman.*

After the Friday night shooting spree, the hospital had given us the boot – every last one of us --and High Plains Medical Center shut its doors. *Wild West Today*, dubbed it "The High Plains Massacre," but ten days later another shoot-out snatched the headlines, and we became just another notch in the ragged holster of American history.

Another few days, maybe a week, and the recent shootings were completely forgotten in the nightmare of the upcoming election. Bully Ratzer was promising to "Make the West Wild Again," while the incumbent, Marjorie Bledsoe, whose voice was shrill as a schoolmarm, wanted to overturn the Guns-for-All Guarantee and the Chinese Exclusion Act. I honestly didn't care who won, I just wanted it to be over.

In a futile attempt to disarm the nightmares, I had spent the days and weeks following the hospital shooting (now down-graded from a Category 4 Massacre) in a self-medicated, whiskey-and-weed induced torpor. I hadn't gone to my friend's memorial service, I hadn't gone to the candlelight vigil held for the victims, and I had failed the Emergency Sharpshooter Response course required for my nursing recertification. My kids had been expelled from school for truancy and I didn't even know it, so shit-faced was I.

*

It was Tonto who rescued me. Tim Rhodes, that is; the former TICU charge nurse at High Plains Medical Center. Tonto got us both per-diem gigs – temporary work at the medical center across town. Wellmart. Night shift, Emergency Department. I was desperate enough to do anything – even Emergency. Even night shift. Even Wellmart.

Rhodes was the quiet, self-assured type. Proud of his Indian ancestry, he wore moccasins and kept his long hair, gray at the temples, in a braid. Tonto and I had worked together for three years, yet we hardly knew each other outside of the trauma unit, and I wondered why he hooked me up with the gig when he might have asked any number of unemployed nurses.

*

Our first shift was a Saturday night. The Indian and I were thrown in cold. There was no orientation for hired guns like us. A busy charge nurse pointed to the crash carts and the medication dispensers, issued our access codes, then threw us to the wolves. Of course, as temp nurses, Tonto and I were given the shit patients. Standard procedure. But we dealt with it, uncomplainingly. To tell you the truth, it was nice to be working again.

*

Hospitals aren't that different, one from the next, and Emergency Rooms work pretty much the same all across the West. People love to complain about ERs. Give them a chance and they always relate horror stories, mostly about how long they had to wait and how nothing was done for them. Yet the fact that they came out alive says something. You don't go to the ER for a shave and a haircut.

My first patient of the night was Cindy, a thirty-six- year old barmaid at the Wrangler Saloon. Cindy came in with a sudden onset of lower right quadrant abdominal pain. I knew right away this would be a long work-up because abdominal pain is a mixed bag. It can be caused by an obstruction, a GI bleed, an ectopic pregnancy; it can be appendicitis, a pulled muscle, peritonitis, PID, or plain old gas.

The doctor was busy in the next room trying to save the life and larynx of a twelve-year-old who had accepted a social media sword-swallowing challenge (with the expected result). Knowing Doc would be tied up awhile, I drew Cindy's blood and collected a urine sample and sent them off to the lab. Then I got my first drunk of the night, apparently one of the regular customers; he knew all the other nurses by name. This was more or less a babysitting assignment, but drunks can get into trouble in the ER. They can fall and break their neck, they aspirate on their own vomit, they can even die on you.

It had been several years since I had worked in the Knife & Gun Club, a.k.a. Emergency Department, Emergency Room, or ER as it has been long referred to as. But I knew what I was in for. ERs are situations of controlled chaos, especially on the night shift.

Working ER is kind of like playing a game. A sick game. Here's how it's played: Patients come in randomly and the object is to get rid of them – either admit them to the hospital or send them home – as quickly as possible. You get extra points (and better social media reviews) if you keep them alive and relieve their suffering while giving them a "positive customer experience." In the ER, we use wits and skills to defeat the opponent. But unlike a game, when Death scores in the ER, there aren't any time-outs or replays. After twenty or thirty minutes of coding a pulseless patient, when the Doc looks at the clock and calls it, the game's over.

The deaths of strangers stay with you like a chronic, low-grade infection. Each loss of life affects you deeply, maybe even on a cellular level. But you don't even realize it at the time. You're just trying to keep the fuckers alive and satisfied. You're just trying to send them home.

Enough morbid philosophy. I was glad for the gig; I'd be making good money here. No bennies – but who needs PTO or health insurance? Retirement? Fuck it; pensions are for snowflakes. If you can't stand the heat, get out of the kitchen. It's high stakes in this poker game and winner takes all. Me? I'm struggling right now, but hey, I've got my rights. Not healthcare rights, not reproductive rights, not education rights – but I've got my gun rights. A Gatling gun in every home – let's make the West wild again.

*

"You're new around these parts," the ER doc said, handing me a chart. She squinted against the garish florescent lights, sizing me up.

"Kit Carson, RN," I said. "I'm a hired gun. I work for the Agency."

"Ruth Halliday," she said, touching the brim of her slouch hat. "Are you Mr. Barker's nurse?"

I nodded.

"He needs blood gasses."

"It's as good as done," I said. Actually, it *was* done. I had already drawn them and sent them to the lab, anticipating the order. Doc's the head honcho, but in Emergency we work as a team.

Doctor Ruth Halliday was a scowling, taciturn woman in worn-down boots and leather chaps that had seen some hard riding. She was an old buffalo soldier, I could see, from the medal-of- honor on her vest. I would grow to trust her and respect her, if not exactly like her. Halliday knew her shit, she could rope, ride, and brand with the best. She knew how to keep those ponies rollin', rollin'. Like the old ER doc's ballad goes,

Move 'em on, head 'em up
Head 'em in, cut 'em out
Get 'em out of my ER,
Rawhide!
Send 'em to the floor
Kick 'em out the door
Come morning we'll be living high and wide...

*

Half past midnight, I needed to pee, but the stampede was on: We were swamped with Saturday night bar fights, knife fights and random shootings. In came the broken bones and kidney stones; chest pains and migraines, common colds and psychiatric holds, overdoses and halitosis -- all seeking refuge and relief inside Wellmart's hallowed halls. No time to eat, no time to piss, but we were gittin' 'er done. Setting bones, suturing wounds, sedating psychotics.

It wasn't until quarter past four in the morning that we finally got a little breather. (Note: Nurses never say the "Q" word while on duty. *Ever*. To utter the word Q-U-I-E-T is bad luck and guarantees that all hell will break loose. It's one of the first things a brand-new nurse learns when she starts her first job.)

Zero Four-Thirty. My drunk was tucked in and sleeping soundly, his bag of yellow nearly finished infusing. I was restocking my rooms when Tonto appeared with a cup of coffee in hand. Smelled good, too, burnt though it was.

"You got a minute?" he said.

I knew what he meant – a little break on the ambulance ramp where we could get our nicotine fix. My heart did a little skip and jump, like a girl playing hopscotch. I've always thought Tonto was kind of hot. For an older guy, that is. Yeah, I had a minute. Maybe more.

*

I bundled up in my duster and neckerchief, my hat pulled down against the biting wind. Tonto slipped a motorcycle jacket on over his scrubs, tied a bandana tied around his head. We stood outside the ambulance entrance sharing the coffee, passing the Marlboro between us.

"What do you ride?" I asked.

"A Sportster," he said.

"I hear you're badass with a bow and arrow," I said. "Is that true?"

He shrugged. "Come to the archery range with me sometime and you can make up your own mind." Tonto had a reputation with a bow and arrow, but I knew nothing at all about Tim Rhodes, the man behind the myth. In the hospital, everybody's got a nickname, a persona, an avatar. Mine's Kit Carson. We don't put our real shit on our badges in case some patient or family member decides to get a little too friendly and stalk us. Or has a vendetta against us.

"So how are you holding up, Kit?" Tonto spoke quietly, his voice, matter-of-fact. But I knew what he was getting at; he was poking at my vulnerable spot, probing that festering wound. My best friend had been killed in the hospital shooting, accidentally shot by one of the other nurses.

I didn't answer. Tonto took a drink of coffee, passed me the cup. The simple gesture made my eyes sting.

"You okay?"

"I'm alive," I quipped. I didn't want Tonto or anybody else see me cry. *Toughen up, buttercup.*

"Yeah, me too," he said. "We're both alive. We should make the most of it."

Suddenly desire surfaced like a joker in the deck of cards that were my emotions. A roll in the hay with Tonto might be just what I needed.

But that too passed. We made small talk – the weather, the news. I wanted to talk about things that mattered. The meaning of time and the universe. My feelings. My hopes and dreams. Neh. Couldn't bring myself to do it. So much easier to repeat slogans and sound-bites. To talk like we text, in smiley faces and emojis.

I drew the last of the cigarette and crushed it out on the icy pavement under the heel of my boot. The wail of a train whistle passing through town cut through my soul. Hearing that sound always made me wish I was on that train, any train, heading somewhere, anywhere. I glanced at my watch; it was time to go back inside and finish the shift.

Tim passed me the last swig of coffee, cold now. I drank it like I was dying of thirst.

Nearby, the sound of squealing tires. Suddenly, there it was – a black livery hauling ass up the ramp. Oh shit; looks like trouble.

The car screeched to a halt, the rear door opened and a body tumbled out onto the pavement at our feet. A bruised and beaten body, unconscious and entirely naked but for the tassel on her left nipple. The car didn't wait but instead drove off, the rear door still open.

"Back to work, Kemosabe," Tonto said.

Down on our knees we went.

"No breath, no pulse," I said, fumbling for my pocket mask. Being closest to her head, I got the airway. Tonto, already astride her torso, his stacked palms on her sternum, two fingers-width up from the xiphoid process, right between those magnificent silicone breasts.

"Hell's bells, it's Stormy Wether," said Tonto, sucking in his breath.

"You *know* her?" I said, then blew into the pocket mask. Her chest rose and fell compliantly.

He shot me a look as he pumped, circulating my breaths through her body. "Are you kidding me? Every man in town knows Stormy Wether. Or at least knows *of* her. She's renowned for her choreography."

"Her choreography?"

"She's a dancer down at the O.K. Corral." Tonto finished the cycle of chest compressions and paused while I gave the celebrity two more breaths.

The O.K. Corral was the kind of establishment most women didn't go to, unless they worked there. Although I was told a woman owned it.

"Is she gonna make it?" I heard a young voice say.

I looked up to see a scantily-dressed girl standing nearby, hugging herself for warmth. She had long bare legs, a knife tucked snugly into a garter belt high on her left thigh. Cheap flashy spurs on fuck-me boots.

"Please save my sister," the girl said, her teeth chattering. "She's all I've got in the world."

Tonto called a code on his phone, and within ninety seconds flat we had all the sharpshooters out on the ramp. Doc Halliday and the A Team to the rescue. A respiratory therapist with a bag valve mask relieved me of my duties; Tonto continued with compressions. We got Ms. Wether on a backboard, through the doors and into Trauma Room #1.

"V-tach, 150. No pulse."

"Let's get some saline going. Type and cross for two units. What's the story?"

"I've got 14-gauge in. Running normal saline, wide open."

"Arrived unconscious, signs of trauma to head and thorax. Possibly assault with a blunt object."

"Continue chest compressions. Hyperventilate and stand by with suction, please. Get me a curved blade and a 7.5 ET tube, let's get her tubed."

"Portable X-Ray standing by."

The entire team worked together following ACLS protocol. It was a beautiful thing to behold.

*

The girl who called herself sister had followed us in and was peeking around the curtain. Her face was badly bruised. I know a fist to the face when I see one. I took her into the adjoining room and pulled the blue curtain closed.

"What's your name, honey?"

"Balmy," she says.

"Barmy?"

"Balmy," she corrected. "Balmy Wether. It's my stage name; I'm a dancer."

Stormy and Balmy Wether. Clever branding, you've got to admit.

"Have you seen me on social media? I've got over five thousand followers on my channel."

"Balmy, that pretty face of yours took quite a punch. Let me have a look."

"I'll be fine," she said, turning away. "It's my sister I'm worried about."

I got her a cold gel pack from the refrigerator, wrapped it in a washcloth. "Here, put this on your eye, it'll help." She flinched when I touched her. "Now then, tell me what happened tonight."

She removed the gel pack to look at me from behind a dark curtain of bangs. Oh, those eyes, those puffy, purple eyes! I assured her the swelling would go down and the bruising would fade, but I wondered to myself if the youthful light would ever return or if she could even remember her innocence.

I had danced for a man, once. My ex. Did a couple of suggestive moves holding onto the poster of our conjugal bed. He had asked me to and I obliged him, feeling rather silly. I remember how excited he had become, the power I seemed to have over him at that moment. Men are strange creatures; normally strong but weak when it comes to their desires.

Balmy wiped a trickle of blood from her upper lip with her finger. "They came into our dressing room after the show. After the bar closed down."

"Look, honey," I said. "We should call the law. Whoever did this to you, they need to be caught and punished."

"No." She was adamant. "You can't do that."

"Why? Are you in some sort of trouble?"

"Yeah," she said with a dry laugh. "You could say that. My whole life has been trouble. But if you call the dawgs my sister is dead, I'm dead, we're both dead."

My skin tingled hearing the calm certainty in her voice.

"How old are you, Balmy?"

"Twenty," she said.

"You mean sixteen?" I countered.

"I'm old enough to know what men want and how to give it to them," she huffed, hand on hip.

My eyes stung with a burst of sympathy for her. I remembered myself at that age – half child, half woman. "Look, Balmy, I'm on your side. My name's Kit. I'm a nurse; I've got your back."

She met my eyes and we had a pact.

"So tell me more about what happened. Who were these men, do you know?"

"Bully Ratzer's guys."

"Sheriff Ratzer?"

She nodded.

"You're telling me Sheriff Ratzer assaulted you?"

Her eye roll said *Duh*, like only a teenager can. "Not Ratzer himself. His thugs. You know, his posse?"

"Why?"

She snorted, impatiently. "Why do you think?"

"At your age you should be babysitting and barrel racing," I said. "Junior Rodeo. Have you thought of joining the Westernaires? The Prairie Scouts?"

She stuck her bottom lip out in a sullen pout. "Don't be so parental."

"I don't mean to be. I can't help it. I've got kids of my own."

"Besides, I make good money performing. Stormy says we'll be real movie stars one day."

I felt disheartened even though she probably made more money than I did. "How much – never mind, don't tell me. The money's not important. Tell me what happened."

"Ratzer's a good customer. A real good customer. Stormy had a special thing going with him, but a few months ago he gave Stormy an envelope of cash; I saw it myself. And he had her sign an agreement, some legal document, and she promised to never say a word about what went on between her and Bully. For a couple of weeks, we were living large. Room service, new clothes, a trip to San Francisco. Then the money ran out and Stormy said it wasn't right to keep silent. On account of Ratzer running for governor. She said the people have a right to know the truth about him and that piece of paper she signed wasn't worth a damn."

"Sit down and let me have a look at your face. You could have a fractured orbital bone. We should at least do an X-ray. And that laceration on your chin, that could use some stiches."

"No," she said. "I don't want my name in the records. I've got to get out of here, find someplace to hide."

"But you're underage. And you're the victim of abuse. I'm obligated to report that."

"You call the law, nurse, and I'm dead."

"Look, I'll do everything I can to protect you. You're safe here in the hospital."

But the girl knew better than I did. "No. I'm not. They're here, Ratzer's goons are here, they followed us."

"Here?" I drew my piece and looked around warily.

"Hey, what's with the gun?" she demanded. "I thought nurses and doctors were supposed to save people, not shoot them. What about the Hippocratic oath?"

"Well, it's complicated," I said. "We have to protect ourselves and our patients. This is the Wild West, you know?"

"I don't buy that."

I put the pistol back in its holster. "So how many of them are there?"

"Two men, maybe three. I don't remember, not clearly. They had masks on. Two of them have thick, hairy arms and little peckers. I bit one of them on his wrist and drew blood."

"You saw their genitals?"

She blinked slowly. "In my line of work, I see a lot of them."

"Yeah, me too."

"Well, I guess we've got that in common," she said. Her smile was a flash of tiny pearls.

"My sister, she's going to be OK, isn't she?"

Just then my phone buzzed, alerting me to a new patient. I pulled it out of my pocket and read the text to see what I was getting. An S.O.B. (that's shortness-of-breath, not son-of-a- bitch) -- and when I looked up, Balmy was gone. *Vamoose*. Nowhere to be seen.

*

I started to assess the S.O.B. – an elderly rancher with emphysema. Took his history, asked all the pertinent questions. Listened to his lungs, his heart, called for a chest X-ray. His wife was with him, silver-haired and gnarled as an old tree branch, likely just as tough.

"Have a seat, Ma'am. Doc Halliday will be in as soon as she Is able."

Going back to the trauma room, I found the team had Stormy intubated, stabilized and was preparing to send her to surgery. Doc suspected a ruptured spleen and other internal injuries. Sinus tach at a rate of 118, blood pressure 90 over 62. The room was trashed, but the patient, alive. I felt a small sense of satisfaction. And something else. Gratitude, maybe?

O.R. sent their own people down to transport Stormy to Surgery. They showed up unannounced, in their green scrubs and booties, bonnets over their Stetsons, and surgical masks covering their mustachios. Not bothering to wait for report, they wheel her away.

I looked around the room, it's trashed like only a trauma room after a code can be. Oh, but wait -- they forgot her patient belonging bag. The only thing inside it was the one tassel, all she had on when she arrived, but it was her tittie tassel, just the same. I wrote her name *Stormy Wether* in a black marker on the outside of the bag.

"Will you cover for me?" I asked Tonto who came in to help me clean up the room. "I'm going to run this to Surgery."

"Wait, Carson," Doc Halliday said, handing me a printout. "Take these lab results up too, please. They just came through."

"Go on, Kit, I've got your back," Tonto said.

"Where *is* Surgery?" I asked, feeling stupid. I had never been beyond Wellmart's Emergency Department.

"Basement," Halliday barked, leaving the room to see to the next patient. "Underground, level two," she said over her shoulder.

Snatching up the plastic bag, I hurried to catch up with the patient. She should have a nurse in attendance. Down the hallway, I saw the surgery techs inside the elevator, the gurney with Stormy Wether between them. I could hear the monitor beeping.

"Wait!" I called to them, but the elevator door closed.

I made for the stairwell, skipping steps, thinking to catch them when they got off the lift two floors below. I didn't count stepping on something – a needle cap? a pen? a bullet casing? Whatever it was, it rolled under my boot and I did a little hoedown trying to keep my footing but ended up falling, twisting my ankle as I went down hard. A sharp pain told me it was probably sprained. Damn! Gingerly, I pulled my foot out of the boot and sure enough, the ankle was already swelling. Responding quickly, I wrapped it with surgical tape – I always carry a roll of it on hemostats clipped to my scrub top. I'm nothing, if not prepared. Then I put my boot back on and hobbled the rest of the way down to Level II Underground.

The elevator was empty. Damn.

I followed the signs to Surgery, limping along like Hopalong Cassidy. My ankle was shooting sparks, but I gritted my teeth and kept going. Outside of the double doors marked

Surgery

I mashed on the automatic opener – but nothing happened. Pulled out my phone to call them – but there was no signal down here. I knocked on the door and heard the intercom crackle.

"Surgery. State your business."

"I'm Kit Carson from the ER. I've got belongings for the patient we just sent you."

The doors swung open to allow me in. A young male clerk behind the desk looked at me curiously.

"From Emergency, are you? Well, that's great, but where's the famous pole dancer? I hear we're about to get a little stormy weather down here."

"She isn't here?" I said, ignoring his innuendos. "That's impossible. I saw her in the elevator two minutes ago. She should be here by now."

"Sounds to me like you lost your patient, Nurse Carson."

"But your people from Surgery came and got her. I was there, I saw them."

"You're mistaken, pardner. We didn't send anybody. We're understaffed; it's just the on-call team here." He grinned. "I think you better go find that stripper. Our guys are scrubbed and ready."

Confused, I turned to leave, still clutching the bag with Stormy's tassel in it. Seeing a wheelchair by the door, I plopped down in the seat.

"Borrowing this rig," I said.

The clerk shrugged. "Ride 'em cowgirl." He turned back to his work.

"Hi ho Silver." I spun the wheelchair around and wheeled out. Which way should I go? Where could they have gone?

Hospital basements are creepy, especially late at night. They might be your best bet in a tornado, but without windows or doors to the outside world it was gloomy as the catacombs down here. All the heavy emotions felt throughout the hospital – fear, pain, grief – have to go somewhere. Maybe they sink like cold air. I could feel them now, a damp cloud; a miasma of sadness.

Halfway down the long corridor, I stopped, got my phone out and tried to call Tonto, but I didn't have a signal down here in the transverse colon of Wellmart's bowels. Seeing a few dots on the waxed hallway floor, I leaned over in the chair for a better look. Blood. Fresh blood, not quite dry. I rolled along, found some more. A trail of blood leading me where? Whose blood? Stormy's? That didn't make sense. She wasn't bleeding except internally. Whose blood?

The trail stopped at the end of the hall. There were two doors on either side. One said

Engineering

From within I could hear the low rumbling hum of the machinery; I could feel the vibration in my bones. I looked through the window. It was dark inside and the door was locked.

The door across the hall was a solid, windowless door with weather sealing. A plaque on the wall next to it said:

Pathology Cold Storage

No Admittance except authorized personnel

Deeming myself authorized, I turned the handle and to my surprise the door opened easily. I rolled the wheelchair inside. It was icy cold and smelled of formaldehyde.

Feeling uneasy, I drew my gun from the holster and released the safety. Thought I heard a scuttling. Rats? It was a lab so maybe there were lab rats. Maybe they did testing or experiments down here.

I felt around and found the light switch on the wall behind me. Florescent overheads whined, flickered erratically a few times, then went out altogether. Must be a bad ballast, I thought. But there should be more lights somewhere. Propping the door open with the wheelchair, I got up, walking slowly on my ankle, wincing from the pain. Found my pocket penlight and looked around at what appeared to be a large storage room. Kind of cluttered, for a lab. It looked more like a storage room, with unused equipment stacked against the wall -- sterilizers, autoclaves, centrifuges, coolers. Boxes of petri dishes, solvents, stains, and cell culture media. On the bench, trays of scalpels and disposable knives laid out. I picked one up and pocketed it; they're handy to have.

Heard a muffled sound, a scuffling, and a little squeak from the rodents. They're active at night, I've heard. Or maybe they were complaining of the cold; it felt like a damn refrigerator in here.

I switched the light off, put it back in my pocket. Now holding my gun in both hands, I looked around me, hyperaware, casing the room like they do in the movies. I inched my way deeper into the dark space, my ankle protesting with every step. I shivered, but was it from the cold or from fear? A few steps more...

My eyes began to adjust to the dark. Just ahead, gurneys – a row of them, like horses tied to the hitching post. Six, to be exact. I hobbled closer, my stomach tightening and the hair on my arms standing up as I realized where I was. The gurneys had bodies on them. This was the cold storage holding area for Wellmart's dead patients. I was in the hospital morgue.

Even with her face covered by a sheet, I recognized Stormy by her breasts, still pointing skyward, firm and proud as the Grand Tetons. With one hand I yanked back the sheet to see her face, drained of all color except for her permanently tattooed lips, resplendently red. I refused to believe she was dead – she had been transported out of the ER alive and stable only five minutes ago. Reflexively, I shook her shoulder, cold but not stiff.

"Stormy!" I hissed.

Stormy did not respond. I leaned close and turned my head, listening and feeling for breath on my cheek, but my own face was numb from the cold. Laying my gun down next to her head, I opened her airway with a jaw thrust, pinched off her nose and delivered two breaths, my lips covering hers, watching her chest rise and fall, rise and fall. Then I felt for a carotid pulse. The portable heart monitor had been turned off, but it was still sitting between her ankles at the foot of the cart. There was an IV pole and the bag of normal saline was still dripping into her vein. What the fuck? Who did this? Ratzer's men?

Balmy had been right, of course. They were here in the hospital. It must have been them behind the surgical masks. Maybe they had Balmy.

Just then I heard the squeaking sound, louder. I sucked in my breath as the corpse on the next gurney writhed under the sheet. Pushing Stormy's gurney aside, I went to the moving corpse, flung off the sheet and found Balmy, gagged and bound to the side rail. With my trusty bandage scissors, I cut the tape across her mouth. She spit out a wad of gauze and gasped for breath.

"Look out! He's got my knife!"

I never even saw him. If I had, or if I had sensed his presence, I might have throat-chopped him or smashed his balls with an awesome kickbox move. Too late, I ducked – but the assailant had me by the hair, yanked me up against him, the cold steel blade pressing against my neck. Instinctively, I froze, not daring to breathe. Too late, my martial arts training kicked in. *Feign submission. Distract opponent.*

"Please, mister, call the doctor," I whispered, sinking against his bulk, raising my arms in a gesture of surrender, then anticipating a momentary shift in his attention, I grabbed his wrist at my neck – the thick, hairy wrist – pulling it down against my chest, rotating the blade outward. Next I tried to pivot under the assailant's arm, like Master Bunn taught us, but it wasn't happening. This thug had me smashed against the gurney with his bulk, I wasn't going anywhere. So I chomped down on his arm like I was biting into an ear of corn, and he dropped the knife alright, but the next thing I knew I was on the floor and this fat fucking ox was on top of me. I couldn't breathe. Why had I stopped jiujitsu after earning a white belt? I cursed myself for being such a dilettante, for not following through with anything. Except nursing. I'm a good nurse, a damn good nurse.

I remembered, with dismay and remorse, my weapon. I hadn't put the pistol back in my holster, but instead, had laid it on gurney when I tried to revive Stormy – for the second time that night. You can't be a good nurse with a gun in your hand.

I could hear the rattle of the side rails as Balmy, still bound, struggled against a second

attacker. "No!" she blurted out, followed by muffled curses and grunts.

In desperation, I tried to scream but it came out a whisper. I couldn't breathe. Like a mule, I drew my knees up and kicked out, trying to buck him off. If only I could get off my back and onto my side, if only I could breathe! I fought the wave of panic crashing over me.

Wait until he makes his next move, I heard Master Bunn say calmly in my mind. I prepared myself to take advantage of the any change. I knew I had to be quick and sure. Sure enough, he shifted his weight to grab my wrists, and as soon as he did, I pulled my arms in close to my body, twisting my torso to one side. My arms were now free, but he swung, his fist hitting the side of my face. My ears rang, darkness closed in, and I fought to stay conscious.

"Drop it!"

It was Halliday's voice, was I imagining it?

"Right now, you sons-a-bitches." She stood in the doorway, backlit by the lights from the corridor. Guns drawn, slouch hat pulled low over her brow, stethoscope looped around her neck. For a long moment no one moved.

Then came the snap crackle of pistol fire from the goon by Balmy and Halliday stumbled back, clutching her shoulder, collapsing into a stack of crates. It all went down with a crash of breaking glass.

I felt the man on top of me move; I drew in a breath and struggled to get up, but his hand slammed my head back against the floor. The room seemed to tilt and whirl. Sparks rained down behind my eyes; shooting stars, like arrows, fell out of the sky. I thought I saw Tonto's face above me, up in the clouds. It was Tonto's face, yes, but streaked with war paint. Was I dying?

I fought against the delirium, struggled to stay awake. Heard a chilling, unearthly war cry pierce the air, then *Thwop Thwop*. The man on top of me slumped over like he was suddenly exhausted. I heard the last breath leave his body in a sigh. Squirming to get out from under him, I felt his hot, spurting blood and saw a well-placed arrow deep in the side of his neck. The other attacker was face down on top of Balmy, an arrow shaft sticking out of his cervical spine.

Tonto looked down from the duct space overhead, a ceiling tile removed. He hung from a pipe, then dropped down soft as a cat in his moccasins, bow in hand. His torso was bare and hairless; a quiver strapped to his back. He knelt over me, his dark eyes peering into mine.

"I'm alive," I panted. "Balmy. Help her. Halliday's been hit."

“I’m able,” Doc said as she staggered through the broken beakers and petri dishes, gripping her left shoulder. “It’s only a scratch.” She made her way to Stormy’s side, feeling for a pulse; I struggled to my feet, head ringing, to assist.

Tonto freed Balmy from her restraints and left her assailant in her place on the gurney, covering him with the blood-stained sheet. Just then the dancer stirred and mumbled, “Will somebody bring me a goddamn blanket? It’s freezing in here!”

*

We rushed Stormy up to the chopper pad, where a chopper was waiting. Halliday had called for an emergency air transport for Stormy (under the alias of Nellie Smith) to Dodge City Trauma Center, beyond Ratzer’s reach. For the moment, she was safe. But we had our work cut out for us, to expose the sheriff and bring him to justice. The dead men we left in the morgue, a coroner’s case that would either be investigated or covered up, depending on Razer’s influence.

Back in the ER, we patched up Halliday’s wound before the day shift started to straggle in. She was lucky; the bullet had missed both artery and bone.

*

07:30.

Tonto walked us to my ride, parked in the North Forty. Clearly the law in this town could not be trusted; Balmy had to lay low until Ratzer was exposed. She was to bunk up with me and the kids until she could be reunited with her sister in Dodge City. In the meanwhile, I figured she could babysit my kids and study for her G.E.D.

“I want to keep an eye on you,” Tonto said. “We can’t be too careful. Don’t know how many men Ratzer has working for him.”

I told him where I lived.

*

I cancelled my shift that evening; my ankle was swollen like a fence post. Scrounged the cupboards, found a single can of pork and beans for Wyatt, Cassidy, and Balmy to share for supper. I collapsed in front of the television to binge on *Smokin’ Guns, Season Three* on DVD, the cable having been shut off last week. But the throaty rumble of a motorcycle interrupted my plan.

"It's the Indian," Balmy said, peering out the window. "He's here."

The engine stopped, and a moment later the doorbell rang.

"Let him in," I said, my heart knocking.

What luck, I thought. Tim Rhodes standing in my living room in his bike leathers – with Chinese take-out, a six pack of beer, and a bundle of sage under his arm.

"I just stopped by to make sure you all were safe. Thought you'd want to know, I spoke with Doc Halliday. Stormy reached Dodge City safely and just got out of surgery. A successful splenectomy. She's in stable condition."

After Tonto saged us and cleansed the room, we all sat cross-legged on the floor, our laps for a table, feasting on Happy Family, beef and broccoli, noodles and rice from Hop Sing's Kitchen. Balmy soon fell asleep on the couch, fast and hard like only a teenager can. Tonto played a few hands of Faro with Wyatt and Cassidy while I took a hot bath. Then it was bedtime for the kids. Tonto took his leave, putting on his leather jacket and goggles.

"Good night, Kemosabe. Get some sleep, I'll call you tomorrow."

I watched through the window as he drove his motorcycle into the moonrise. Tucked the kids in, turned the lights out, covered Balmy with a spare blanket. Only then did I eat my fortune cookie, saving the message until I had swallowed the last crumb.

THREE

SUNDAY NIGHT KNIFE & GUN CLUB

Sunday night
Kit Carson, RN
The winter had been a long one and it was not yet spring. I was driving to work, late again, mind busy, overflowing with to-do lists, should-have-done lists, the occasional misplaced memory blowing through like a random tumbleweed. Last week's lynching, the way the dead man's boots twitched, a dog dreaming. Tonto's forearms, his concentration when he drew his bow (a warm tingling down south, picturing his muscles tensed, the arrow poised). Those men we left for dead down in the hospital morgue. Random images. Floaters. Blink, they're gone and a new day's shit pile to deal with.

My pickup, a Dodge Power Wagon, galloping along with never a word of complaint. Oil change and new tires all the way around – that put a dent in my charge card but I felt indestructible in that badass machine. Love my sexy set of wheels, she's fully restored (except for a broken window and glove box latch) and only five more years of payments! Lately, a family had taken up residence in the back, hanging a blue plastic tarp over the bed, tent-like, to keep out the sleet and snow. Beneath the tarp a string of lights lent a bit of cheer to the situation. I'd never actually seen any of them, they were invisible to me, but I couldn't help notice little scraps of their existence. A glove dropped in the snow. An empty water bottle under the wheel. Sometimes when I got into the cab I smelled green chili and pork simmering in the back. But I kept my blinders on. Hell, I had enough to worry about looking after my own. Those people were no concern of mine.

Traffic in town was heavy that Sunday night, a regular stampede. Used to be Sundays were slow but lately there'd been a rush of interlopers to the city of High Plains and the whole Front Range. They came for the silver, they came for the gold, they came for the oil and gas, they come for the dope. It's boom or bust baby, and High Plains was booming. Me, I'm practically a native, I've got the bumper sticker to prove it.

I stepped on the gas and was making up for lost time when I saw a lasso of blue and red lights in the rearview. Shit damn hellsafire, I don't need this.

Braking and signaling (and hoping my lights weren't burned out), I pulled off the highway onto the shoulder. What will I say? Cops and nurses, we supposedly have an affinity or something. I'll tell him I'm late for my shift and give him the look, you know the look. Maybe I'll get lucky and he'll let me off. Unless... What if it's one of Bully Ratzer's deputies? What if he knows the dancer Balmy Wether is under *my* protection, that she's living under my roof, babysitting my kids, taking online courses to get her high school diploma? What if he knows she's ready to rat out the sheriff of High Plains?

A flashlight in my face, a tap on the window. "Roll 'em down, cowgirl."

My stomach, in knots. "It won't roll down," I said, speaking loudly, so he could hear me through the glass. "It's broken. The window's broken."

"Keep your hands where I can see 'em."

I gripped the steering wheel to keep my hands from shaking.

"Now open the door. Easy does it, nice and slow. Keep your right hand on the wheel."

I did as he bid.

"Atta girl."

The hombre was tall. Over six feet, I reckoned. I couldn't even see his face way up there.

"Now, let me see your papers. Driver's license, registration, proof of insurance. No sudden moves, cowgirl. "

The click of a safety being released triggered my heart rate to 130 sinus tach, with a couple of PVCs thrown in. I could accurately gauge its rate and rhythm because heartbeats are my business. Critical care and emergency nursing, my expertise. Swallowing hard, I reached over to open the glove box and the damn door fell off in my hand. Of course it did; I had forgotten about the broken latch. Out poured an avalanche of shit – old gasoline receipts, unopened pack of tampons and an empty pack of Marlboros, CPR pocket mask, a box of nine millimeter bullets and a wad of paper napkins from Waco Taco. Somewhere amid the detritus of my road life I found what I was looking for. Handed over my paperwork and awaited my fate.

He shone the flashlight on my card. "Your insurance is expired."

"Well, actually it's not. I just keep forgetting to replace the card."

"Ma'am, this card is ten years old."

"It is? But really I do have car insurance, officer."

"Yeah? Well, what about health insurance. You got that?"

"Can't afford it. I'm a per diem nurse. No bennies. Gig economy, ya know?"

"It looks like I'm going to have to write you up, cowgirl. Wait here 'til I run this." The lawman went back to his ride. Shit, I am fucked. They're probably done with report by now; I'm liable to get the boot for being late again.

Meanwhile, cars flew by me on the highway. I could just imagine the drivers looking over and seeing me snared by the blue and red lasso, thinking "serves her right" and "better her than me." Altruism is dead.

The cop wasn't gone long, and when he came back he handed me an envelope. "Be careful now, Nurse Carson," he said. "Be real careful. You're being watched."

My stomach tightened, and the skin on the back of my neck tingled. "Thank you, Officer," I said. "I'll be on the lookout." For what, I wondered?

He turned to go then paused, looking over his shoulder. "I see you're carrying undocumented workers."

"I am?" I feigned surprise. "But I've never actually *seen* anyone back there."

The officer touched the brim of his hat. "Well, ma'am, I'll be on my way. Take care now."

He walked off into the moonlight, his boots crunching on the gravel. Got in his ride and waited for me to drive off.

It wasn't until I got to work, parked in the lot, that I dared open the envelope. Right there in the parking garage, I read it under the sickly yellow lights.

You are hereby requested to appear at the Watering Hole Saloon,
Sunday night at 9:00 pm.
Come alone and come armed.
~ *High Plains Vigilantes for American Justice*

My stomach did a flip- flop, my fingertips tingled. Carefully I put the slip of paper back in the envelope and stuffed it inside my Kevlar vest. There must be some mistake. Not to mention, the Watering Hole was such a dive. Only the drovers and the dregs drank there.

Doc Halliday

Dr. Ruth Halliday slipped into the nurses' lounge for a cuppa joe before starting her shift. The little room, the so-called "lounge," (really more of a burrow or a den) was a mélange of ethnic food odors, microwave popcorn, coffee, and something else – what was it? – wet socks? The nurses were a messy lot, but they had coffee. Real brew, an old- fashioned communal coffee pot, which was more than she could say for the doctors' lounge, which actually *was* a lounge, a well-appointed one, but way over in the south wing. Not that anyone thought ER doctors needed a lounge. In the eyes of the head honchos, Emergency physicians were glorified veterinarians. Whatever, she didn't care. She was just putting in her time here. At least in the nurses' den she had her own coffee cup. The nurses had bought it for her last Christmas and filled it with chocolate hearts and candy kisses. They even had it personalized with her name:

Doc Halliday

Badass-est ER Doc in the West

The mug was stained with a little chip out of the handle. Damaged, like the nurses. She loved them. They were almost like family. No, they were family.

Pulling her slouch hat low over one eye, Ruth adjusted her thigh holsters beneath the canvas duster she had taken to wearing and looped the stethoscope around her neck with a practiced flip of her hand. Pushed the swinging door open and went out to face the night.

A glance at the white board in the nurses' station was a preview of the night to come:

Rm. 1 Johnson FLU SX OTD

Rm. 2 Chang Ψ consult

Rm. 3 Miller FUO ADMT RM #602

Rm. 4 Barnes LOLNAD FOS?

Rm. 5 Garcia SOB

Rm. 6 Gonzales R/O FX R radius OTD

Rm. 7 Walsh ETOH BA? (316 Bess 288 Shorty 250 Larry)

The ER hands wrote and spoke a language of initials and acronyms. It was a shorthand and a code as well as a psychological buffer. Must maintain a distance even while we are invading their bodies and minds with fingers, tubes, catheters, sharp instruments, blunt words.

"Howdy, Doc Ruth." Stretch, the EMT, a cocky little cowhand but a good kid; a team player. "Better place your bet on Walsh's BA before the labs come back, ma'am."

The ER staff runs pools, bets on lab results, especially blood alcohol levels; those were the favored game. Were they frequent fliers? If so, there's a baseline BA on them in the medical records and the player places his bet comparing the patient's current LOC with past levels of consciousness. The nurses run this casino, but the docs are inveterate gamblers, everyone knows. Ruth was always game to play along.

OTD on only two rooms. *Out the Door*. Discharged. Treat 'em and street 'em, that's our goal. LOLNAD always a favorite, those sweet little old ladies in no apparent distress. A memory of baking cookies with Gramma flashes through her consciousness except there were no smells of baking cookies to accompany the visual. Instead another scent, a warm chocolate mess but definitely not chocolate chips, she'd wager.

TVs blaring, every monitor in the department tuned to the corporate Wellmart channel, all they could get. Be glad when this election's over, sick of the political stink. Bully Ratzer promising to make the West wild again, guaranteeing freedom and gun rights for all. His ads were all over the media, his face on posters and handbills all over town. Running against the righteously shrill-voiced Marjorie Bledsoe. Maybe she did sell arms to the Arapahos and, yeah, the last Comanche attack happened on her watch, but Ratzer's a lying, thieving, extorting, uneducated bounder. Bad enough he's sheriff – Can't believe he's running for governor. But no way he'll win, not after we expose him. In this country a man's character counts for something.

*

Room 4. Pull on gloves, insert finger into anus, mind far away. Mind divided, split screen. One side, an old white woman's hind end; on the other, Ruth's happy place, a Las Vegas casino, where the piano man plays a lively tune and the smell of whiskey and fine cigars fill the air. In her hand, a royal flush. The hostess with perky boobs brings her drink, her musky perfume has a lingering finish...

On the gurney the patient twisted and bucked like a steer, crying rape. Whoa Nelly, hold still there, we're trying to help you. The nurse struggled to hold the old woman down. Carson, that's her name. Kit Carson. She's the one mixed up in the whole Wether sisters affair.

Ruth extracted her finger, wiped it on the disposable pad and peeled the gloves off, one encased neatly inside the other. She then dropped the wad of latex into the biohazard trash.

"Disempact her, nurse Carson. Clean 'er out real good. Test for occult blood, just for the record, and send her back to the home."

What people don't realize is a fecal impaction can kill you. Slowly. Insidiously. But as surely as a bullet in the brain, shit stuck in the colon can kill. Another life saved. Yippi ty yi yay, get along little doggie, it's your misfortune and none of my own.

Kit

"You're late, Carson," the charge nurse had accused. "Report was finished ten minutes ago."

"Sorry," I said. "I got pulled over by the Law. "

"Sorry don't cut it; it'll be noted on your record. But here's your chance for redemption. Tonight, every shit patient is yours; starting with room 4." She flashed me a jaded smirk. "Oh, and you'll want the heavy duty gloves. Extra long."

That's how I got stuck with the dis-impaction. Halliday, of course, didn't stick around for all of that. Digging out is a nurse's job. A new pack of blue plastic pads, a tube of lubricant, a bag of warm water hanging from the IV pole, I was ready to go.

"Unhand me, bitch!" Little Old Lady cried out, imperious as a queen.

"Whoa there, Nellie! Hold still, this won't take long." One hand on her bony hip, I steeled myself for the task.

"Alexa, play something soothing."

Oh, give me land, lots of land under starry skies above, Gene Autry crooned.

"Alexa, turn up the volume."

Fifteen minutes later, the dirty deed done, I opened a vial of peppermint oil to freshen the air. The descending colon was now glistening pink and empty, and the woman to whom the organ belonged was sleeping. Come morning, this would all be an unpleasant dream for both of us.

I made my exit, carrying a blue bundle of steaming shit in my hands. The hallway was lined with spectators – families of other patients in adjoining rooms – who had undoubtedly heard everything going on behind the curtain. They watched me in horror as I made my way toward the hopper, dumped the load and flushed twice.

Back in the patient's room, Ruth was doing a final check.

"You were invited," she said to me. It was a statement. Definitely not a question.

"I was what?"

She didn't respond but glanced pointedly toward the camera mounted above the door. You couldn't be too careful, there were eyes and ears everywhere.

"Alexa, get me Mr. Smith's medical records. And play *I'm an Old Cowhand*."

When the music started, she spoke in a low, matter-of-fact voice, like she was asking me to open a packet of KY jelly. "You were invited to the watering hole Sunday night. We could use a few good nurses." She pulled a prescription pad out of her pocket, scribbled something, tore it off and gave it to me. *Meet us at the blackjack table at nine, ready to roll*

"It's a shooting club," she said with a look freighted with hidden meaning. "We get together for cards and drinks."

Ruth Halliday, that old buffalo soldier, was a vigilante?

I figured maybe I should go. I wasn't very good at shooting, my marksmanship sucked, but I could stick a vein, any vein, on the first try. Blindfolded, one hand behind my back. If there was a medal for IV sticks, I'd a won it. Good at triage too. Maybe those skills would come in handy. Hopefully they weren't looking for a secretary. I had never been a joiner, my social life was null and void, and I hadn't a clue how to play blackjack. But I had been asked – tapped – by a secret society. It was flattering, it was an honor. I only hoped the dues wouldn't be too high.

Wyatt

He hit PAUSE, freezing the game. His eyes hurt. He was hungry, or bored. Maybe both. Calamity, asleep on the couch next to Balmy, season 36 of *The Gamblers* on the screen. So boring it must have knocked them out. He was lonely but didn't want to wake them, especially not his sister; she would be all needy and want him to make popcorn. Wait – popcorn – good idea. They looked like unborn babies, all fetal together, eyelids fluttering, minds blank. Unidentical twins. Fraternal twins. No, sisternal twins. Except Balmy's not my sister. I don't know how long she's gonna stay with us. I like her – she's hot – even if her face is all fucked up from the beatings.

But something's not right. The hair on the back of his neck prickled. Gun up, make the rounds. Check windows. Check doors and locks. Still, the feeling, the sharp taste in his mouth. I'm the man of the house. Protector.

What's that? Sounds like something's up in the crawl space. Squirrels? A raccoon? Maybe an intruder. The piece, solid in his hand. Safety off, the bitch was ready. Do a visual on every room, check all five. Maybe a minute passed. Maybe more. All quiet.

Fuck! Somebody was knocking at the door! No, not a knock, more like a soft tap-tap-tap. He stood on his toes to look out the peephole but couldn't see anything. Another tap-tap-tap. Just do it, go on. Safety off, he was ready for anything. Ready to squeeze the trigger and blow the sumbitch away.

There at his feet, a puppy. No shit, a real live puppy all shivering and pathetic. As Wyatt bent to scoop it up, he saw the boy standing in the shadows of the porch. His own height. No hat. No fucking hat. Shivering like the puppy. With the door open the wind blew in, swirling through the house. But the boy just stood there. Wyatt thought he looked familiar.

"This your dog?"

"I thought you might want it."

The kid sounded alright. Sounded normal. Wyatt judged him not a threat. The puppy squirmed and he felt a sudden wet warmth against his stomach.

"Come on in," he said, his hands full with puppy and gun. "Take your shoes off; my mom'll have a fit."

The boy removed his off-brand sneakers and lined them up next to the others in the boot tray beside the door. Wyatt put his finger to his lips. Now the gun felt awkward and stupid, but he didn't want to lay it down, not just yet. He motioned for the boy to follow him to his bedroom where he shut the door behind them so they could talk.

"Are you one of the ones who live in the back of our truck?"

The kid nodded.

"What's your name?"

"Mike. What's yours?"

"Wyatt. What are you doing here?"

"Relocating. My dad and my uncle are looking for work."

"What kind of work?"

"Wiring houses 'n stuff. They're electricians."

"You speak good English."

The boy named Mike looked at him, like, duh. "Born in the U.S.A. Same as you."

Wyatt was aware of the puppy, chewing his fingers with tiny, sharp teeth. He could smell his sour puppy breath and his puppy pee on his shirt. "What should we name him?"

Mike shrugged. "What about Cesar?"

"Yeah, that's cool. I think Cesar's hungry. What about you?"

Mike smiled.

"Me too. Let's make some popcorn."

Kit

Hospitals and bars each have their own particular stink. Frankly, I preferred the lived-in smell of a local watering hole. That smoky, whiskey, wet leather and beer-soaked floorboards funk was a welcome change from the hospital's olfactory delights. I'd never spent much time in the company of drinkers, but I'd always wanted to be part of the easy camaraderie, the low society of alcoholics, whores, gamblers, cocaine dealers and piano players who call a bar home.

I sat at the blackjack table, next to Doc; I was in deep over my head after only an hour. The barmaid had just brought another round when my phone vibrated. A text from Wyatt, I read it discreetly under the table.

Mom, can I have a dog?

No. Go to sleep.

I found one by the front door. He was cold.

No dogs, Wyatt.

Mom?

What?

The boy's name is Mike.

What boy?

You know. The boy who lives in the back of the truck.

Don't encourage them! Be safe, keep doors locked, guns loaded! Good Night!

I added a bunch of hearts and zzzzz's to sign off.

Mentally back in the game, but now I had lost my focus and any luck I might have had. I couldn't help feeling out of my element. I didn't even know these people. Well, except for Doc Halliday and Officer True who had pulled me over last week. High rollers, hired guns, and card sharps by the looks of it. I fingered my little stack of chips and tried to concentrate.

The dealer shuffled the cards and began a new session. Wait, what? Graffiti on the cards. Words and cryptic phrases. My assignment was turning up bit by bit on the faces of the cards. A seven of spades with "Balmy" scrawled in pencil. A queen of diamonds said "Stormy Wether in Cheyenne." So this is how it's played! My breath came in gulps but I put on my best poker face. Played a card, was dealt another. The deuce of clubs. Across its face in black ink. *Fold 'em sucker!*

I looked at Doc and she nodded. I stood up, leaving my chips, my cards on the table. "I got you covered," Halliday said. And so I walked out into the cold night, trying to piece it all together, what I was expected to do.

The doctor caught up with me in the parking lot.

"Tonto's got Stormy, he's expecting you at the Hitching Post on Lincoln Avenue. His people have agreed to give the sisters refuge until after the story breaks and Ratzer's taken down. But don't expect it to go smoothly. We have reason to believe the plan's been hacked."

I reached for my keys, a tingle of fear and excitement racing through my arms and legs.

"Wait a minute," Doc said. "I've got some medical supplies. Never know what you're going to run into out there."

Halliday went to her ride and brought back a medical kit, must've weighed twenty pounds. I took a look inside: antibiotics, catheters and ET tubes, enema kits, IV supplies, scalpels, pick-ups, sutures, splints. All the essential drugs, even a flask of whiskey and a bite stick. Hell, with these supplies I could dig out a bullet, deliver a breech calf, or transplant a kidney. I was set.

"Anything else I need to know?"

"There'll be a reporter from the Washington Post with the Indians, to interview the sisters. When this story hits the papers, Bully Ratzer's going down."

From the back of my truck I could hear music. Very faint, but yes, it was definitely mariachi. I fired up the ignition, wondering if Halliday heard it.

"Keep your cell phone handy. Plans could change at any minute." The doctor started to walk back to the bar then paused, looking over her shoulder.

"*Vaya con Dios*, Carson."

Tonto

He had been following the white owl for miles, westward across the plain. Whether the raptor was real in feather and flesh or existed only in his mind's eye, he couldn't say. Didn't matter, it was one and the same. Mile after mile after mile, astride the steel and chrome Indian Chief Dark Horse rumbling through the night, Tim Rhodes, a.k.a. Tonto, rode like the wind along the ancient pathway of his people. I-80. A pathway now paved with asphalt and divided by white slashes, like war paint.

He rode in a trance-like state, unmindful of the biting wind on his cheek, dreaming in the old language, a language he had never been taught yet somehow understood. He was getting aroused, the vibration of his motorcycle between his legs, the woman's arms around him, her warm breasts pressing into his back, her bruised face resting against his shoulder. Couldn't help that. He may be Arapaho, he may be a nurse, but he was a man first and foremost. Not so young anymore, his hair gone to gray, but he was still virile. Was Stormy sleeping, he wondered?

He hoped so. Tonto felt gentle and powerful at the same time. He would fight, he would kill if he had to, though it violated his oath. He was, after all, a nurse. A rogue nurse but still a nurse who lived by the sacred creed. *Do no harm, take no shit*.

Ahead, the white owl circled impatiently, waiting for him to catch up.

The road stretched ahead, rising slightly with each mile. No moon tonight, only starlight, the voices of a million lives, past lives, lives yet to come. Certainly he had entertained fantasies of Stormy, what man hadn't? But now that she was under his protection it was the other female, the one back in High Plains whom he was thinking of. The nurse who called herself Kit Carson, he imagined she had been sent by the spirit Splinter-foot, the huntress born of the hunter's swollen leg. Tonto had been studying Arapaho mythology, having been deprived of it growing up. Splinter-foot lived with her six sisters in a star cluster high overhead, what the dominant culture called the Pleiades or Seven Sisters. Tonto lived close to the stars.

They were at war with Nihancan, the crazy one, the spider trickster, that old enemy of the White Sage People. Nihancan was the white man with the gun. Tonto was only now coming into the fullness of understanding, awareness of his being, his true *being*. White Owl and Splinter-Foot were his spirit guides. His mission unfolded before him. To deliver the dancing woman and her sister to the safety and protection of his people, waiting for him in Cheyenne.

Ahead, the owl flew on like an arrow, time's arrow, and beneath him his ride rumbled on.

Kit

Hauling ass on the highway, heading north. Searching for a radio station, but it's all shit these days. The clutter on the edge of town, never ending. Once endless plains and open range, now condos and swimming pools, outlet malls and superstores, ranchettes and golf courses. They keep coming, all looking for something, for blue sky and purple sage. Everybody wants to be a cowboy, baby. Everybody wants to get high and shoot a gun.

One eye on the rearview, I've got a feeling I'm being followed.

Ratzer's men are everywhere, or so I imagined. It's a damn shame we can't trust our elected public servants.

"Mommy, I'm hungry."

"Hang on, sweetheart. Balmy, would you kindly get her a pop tart? They're in my saddle bag."

I could feel the teenager's eye roll in the dark. She exhaled a sigh of forbearance and reached down on the floor by her feet to oblige me.

"No need to be rude, Balmy. Where are your manners?"

"Yes, *ma'am*."

"No need to be sarcastic either. A little gratitude would be appreciated, thank you." I liked her. She reminded me of me, a few years back. All hair and attitude with tits to match.

It was Balmy who got Stormy to the hospital after the sheriff's goons tried to convince Stormy to keep silent. It was really Balmy who saved Stormy's life. After her operation, the vigilantes had her airlifted to an undisclosed private facility in Kansas to recover. There, she had been given a new identity. But none of us would rest until Bully and his men were behind bars.

From the back seat I could hear the music leaking from Wyatt's earbuds.

"Turn that down, cowboy, you're going to blow out your eardrums."

Amazingly, he complied. Then I heard another sound, a whimpering whine that could only be one thing.

"Is there a dog in my back seat?"

No answer, just another pathetic sound like a small, helpless animal pleading for its life.

"I told you no dogs."

"He needs a home, Mommy," says Calamity. "He lost his family."

Don't look, I tell myself. But I do. One quick glance in the rearview is enough. Oh, that little fucker. So small, so helpless, so stinkin' cute.

"Goddammit, kids. Last thing in the world I need is a puppy chewing my boots. Last thing I need is to step in a puddle in my stocking feet. Last thing I need is another creature depending on me for their very existence." My turn to heave a sigh, which no one comprehended or even heard.

The smell of acetone filled the cab. Next to me, Balmy was painting her nails, her hand splayed out on her denim-clad thigh. Her long dancer's legs folded at impossible angles, her stocking feet on the seat next to her ass. She resembled the letter M. Her hair cascaded over her shoulders. Balmy's been a sex slave who knows how long? I wondered what her real name was but I didn't ask. All of us hide behind our avatars.

"Hey, Balms," said Wyatt from the back seat. "Pass me the pop tarts, bee-atch."

They maligned each other lovingly, like brother and sister.

"Wait a sec, butthead, my nails are wet." She blew on her fingertips like she was extinguishing sixteen birthday candles on a cake. Tossed the box of tarts into the back seat. In the rearview, I saw Wyatt slide open the window and pass the box through to the waiting hand on the other side. So he was feeding them too.

Balmy, finished with her manicure, made a pillow of my saddlebag and fell asleep against the window. It amazed me how quickly she could tune out the world. The kids in the back, the puppy, all quiet. Not a peep. I was in charge; they all trusted me to keep them safe while they slept. Jesusfuckingchrist, the responsibility was overwhelming sometimes. But the hum of tires against the asphalt was liberating. Behind us, the city lights fell away and the darkness swallowed us. Now I could see a scattering of stars through the windshield. One of them was the North Star but which one? The night sky was a revolving map, but I didn't know how to read it. If it wasn't for my phone I'd be lost. Tonto would know. Tonto, on his way to meet us, our paths to intersect. Maybe after the Wether sisters were safely reunited he and I would unite. The thought warmed me as I imagined the details. Mile after mile the highway unfurled.

*

Out of nowhere, headlights were creeping up my ass. I got an odd feeling, I don't know, like I get when a patient who looks stable is fixin' to go south. Call it intuition, call it luck, call it experience. I gave the beast a kick in the gas flanks and sped up to ninety to see if I could lose whoever was tailing me, but they kept up. Then I slowed back down, thinking, what if it's the Law and they're after me for speeding? But there was no lasso of lights, no siren. The hair on my arms stood up. Suddenly I'm scared shitless, I need some help here! Buck up, Carson. Keep your hands on the wheel and your foot on the gas.

Calamity

Was it too late to be someone else? If she went to sleep, might she dream up a new life? Next life she would have a dad like the one in the dollhouse. That dad had gone missing too, it was her fault. *Calamity, keep your toys picked up!* Sad. Suck on the blanket's soft corner. *Close your eyes and go to sleep, Calamity*. Fake sleep. Play dead to survive, that's what they taught in school. Fire drills and shooter drills. Stranger danger, Sharing is caring. When you wish upon a star. ABCDEFG. Wyatt's friend, his family, those Electricans that live in the back of the truck, they'll help us, we'll help them. Just like a real family, a family with a dad or maybe even two.

Balmy

She had somehow lost her memories, maybe left them in a dream. Now she was in a dream, knew she was dreaming. Looking for something or someone. Her sister. Not Stormy but her real sister, possibly her identical twin. She wanted to call out to her, but she couldn't remember her name. She couldn't remember her own name. A door, she opened it, a swinging barroom door, and inside, a mechanical girl on all fours, twisting and bucking for all she was worth. Sign said *Drop a nickel in the Slot to make her Buck*. The next cowboy climbed on. She looked up and smiled, but her face was a cow's skull, bleached white bone, empty sockets for eyes.

"Balmy!"

Now she's grabbing the mechanical girl by the hair, pulling with all her might, struggling toward the surface of the dream. Wanting to breathe.

"Balmy, wake up!"

Kit

"Balmy, you awake?"

She mumbled something from behind the curtain of bleached hair.

"Balmy, wake up. Trouble behind and it ain't Casey Jones."

The teenager unfolded herself, now wide awake.

"Somebody's tailing us. I don't like the looks of it." Was it just some Wyoming cowboy on meth? Or was it one of Ratzer's posse in pursuit?

The lights in my rearview flashed on high beam, nearly blinding me. I signaled, moving over into the slow lane, to allow them to pass, but they followed, staying right up my ass. I tromped my boot on the accelerator, and my Power Wagon leaped like a charger, the speedometer pegged at 110. We charged along the highway, straight as an arrow. I moved back into the fast lane, though there were no cars ahead of me as far as I could see. Fort Collins was now behind us, we were entering the territory's north forty. Gone were the strip malls, the condominium clones, the big box stores. It was like driving into the past, into the real American West. Still, the vehicle behind me kept pace.

"Now hold on in the back, kids, and get ready. I'm fixin' to flip a bitch."

Easing up on the gas, slowing down until I knew I could pull it off, I suddenly veered across the median strip. Up onto two wheels, bouncing on the rough turf, I held my breath until I hit the southbound pavement, finishing my turn. From the back, yeehaws and *arribas* as we flew past the vehicle on our tail, a late model luxury SUV, black or possibly gray, hard to tell. In my rearview, I saw the brake lights as they slowed, probably preparing to make the same maneuver. Turned my headlights off, down-shifted to slow my speed so the brake lights wouldn't show, then drove onto the shoulder, past the guardrail and onto the frontage road, took it to the next overpass, crossed over and headed north again on the east access road, driving like hellfire, no lights. Quite a piece of fancy ridin' if I do say so myself.

"Mommy, I have to tinkle."

"Hold it, Calamity. I'm a little busy here."

"But I've been holding it a long time already."

"Mom, are we there yet?" Wyatt, coming to life again in the back seat.

"We can't outrun these guys forever, they've got a faster horse. Besides, we're low on gas. Balmy, pull up a map, would you? See what our options are. Find some place to lose these losers."

Next to me, Balmy studied the screen in the palm of her hand. In her lap I saw my revolver, locked and loaded. "There's a ghost town ahead to the right. Further right – I mean East – you can pick up 85."

Lights behind us on the frontage road, are you fucking kidding me? I dug my spurs into the floorboard, urging the old Wagon on.

"Or," said Balmy, "there's the sandstone fort ahead, just off the interstate. Maybe we can ambush 'em."

"Text Tonto, tell him to meet us there, pronto. Tell him what to expect. Wyatt, cover your sister. Keep your heads down. But just in case, you better gun up the guys in the back."

Wyatt took the Remington off the gun rack and handed it back through the sliding panel.

The bad guys fired first (they always do.) The sound of bullets ricocheting off the Wagon's flanks.

"Get down and stay down!" I slammed the pedal to the metal, the last bit of speed out of the beast, watching the gas gauge drop almost to E.

My phone pinged with an incoming text.

"Tonto," Balmy announced. "He's on his way."

*

A pop, a lurch, and suddenly it felt like we were driving through a river of sand. Tire blown, probably shot out. Like a bad dream, I fought for control. We were crippled, hobbled, no chance of outrunning them now. I needed a little time, but time had run out.

I smelled gasoline. What the hell? From the back of the truck I heard a loud crash, the breaking of glass. In my mirrors a flash of light followed by the force of an explosion, like a tailwind from hell, followed by an unholy boom.

"Hooray! It's the Electricans," Wyatt called out. I felt a burst of gratitude for the family in the back, the people I had chosen not to see. We were in this together, our lives were all at stake. Firebombs made with recycled bottles and gas from the red can, buying us a little time and sending out a signal of distress. Get the kids to safety, the only thought on my mind. Keep driving. Bumping along on three good tires and a rim, putting distance between us. Ahead, I could see the towering sandstone hoodoos, glowing red in the fire's light, offering their silent protection.

*

We stepped carefully over the bones and broken arrow shafts, shards of booze bottles crunching underfoot, looking for a place to hide. Wyatt and Mike found a snug little cavity in the rock, just above eye level. The kids climbed up, snuggling in like a little wolf pack, the puppy nestled between them. A silver-haired woman with a machete beneath her serape (Mike's *abuela*, I would find out later) stayed with me, guarding the kids. The men (Mike's father and uncle, I would find out later) stayed in the back of the truck, armed with the Remington and an arsenal of knives. We waited. The only sound I heard was the sound my own heart, knocking like a badly tuned engine.

And then they came limping in. No headlights, no taillights, no windshield – just a glittering rim of broken glass. Coughing and sputtering, the vehicle came to a stop about fifty yards from where I had parked the truck. The charred doors swung open and a burst of gunfire rang out, ricocheting off the rocks. The kids, the puppy, the grandma, all remained silent. I crouched outside the cave with my weapon drawn. Long minutes passed with no sound but the wind coming up, a mournful keening.

A whisper overhead, my heart jumped. I turned to look, pointing the pistol clutched between my hands. There on a ledge of rock above me, an owl, its heart-shaped face white in the star shine. We looked at each other, acknowledged each other. Both of us alive, hearts beating, sharing that particular slab of sandstone at that particular moment in time.

And then a new sound. In the distance a vibration like the hooves of a thousand buffalo thundering across the plains. Louder now, closer, the shaking of the earth became a throaty rumble, the sound of a dozen American-made motorcycles.

Tonto

Scattering swiftly, they surrounded the fort, leaving their steel ponies ground-tied and waiting. They were led by an old brave who had studied the ways of his ancestors and served in the occupier's recent wars. Tonto was no warrior, he was a medicine man.

His concern was for Kit and the children, but he also had Stormy to protect, not to mention the dude with the camera, the city slicker-reporter. Tonto didn't feel the lust for revenge in his soul, but he did own a desire to do good and the will to put things right. So many people to protect, it was a burden. But Tonto had a sharp knife, a well-strung bow, and a quiver of steel tipped, carbon fiber arrows. He might not have been quite as quick as he once was, but if anything, he was more experienced and far more sure.

A rapid burst of gunfire ripped through the rocks, it was hard to tell from where it came. His brothers and sisters would need time to evaluate the situation, to pinpoint their targets and get into position. The enemy had superior weaponry, but the Arapaho had strategy and stealth on their side.

"Let me be the bait," Stormy whispered in his ear, tugging his sleeve. "I can distract them for a minute, maybe draw them out of hiding."

Too risky. But she bolted, knowing her own mind, leaving the safety of his protection. Seeing a horizontal slab of rock nearby, she scrambled onto it. Shit. Nothing to do but cover her.

"Shine your light on me, honey," she called out. "Watch me groove."

Tonto swung the bike to face her, switching on the headlamp. Some of his tribe, hidden in the shadows, began a chant, their voices rising in unison. The sandstone amplified the sound until it became a true rock concert. Slowly she began to gyrate, peeling off her shirt one sleeve at a time, pulling her short leather skirt down over her hips and boots, stepping free of it, knowing she was being watched. Squatting, thrusting, spreading her limbs to their best advantage, she rhythmically contorted her near-naked body to the masculine chant as only Stormy Wether could do. Tonto himself was momentarily mesmerized. Meanwhile, under the cover of darkness, the other Arapahos crept in, raising their bows.

Kit

I heard the sound of Indian plainsong rising up from the ground itself. It was both earthy and bone-chilling eerie and the hair on my arms stood up. I kept my eyes alert for movement, ready to blow away anyone coming for my family. If this was to be the end of my world, I would go out in a firestorm, I would protect my kids with my last breath.

Gunfire nearby, instinctively I ducked bullets, and shards of rock went flying by my head. Then silence. The Indians had stopped chanting.

"Well looky here, if it ain't Kit Carson herself."

A man's voice with a Texas drawl. Definitely not Ratzer, who retained his nasal, East Coast twang. The Texan stepped out from behind a hoodoo, all boots, duster, and ten-gallon hat towering over me. I couldn't see his face.

"What do you want?" I spat.

"Hand over the whore. Give me that little bitch or you're all dead."

My blood rose up in rage and defiance. I was fixin' to shoot him, but I knew I only had one chance. My shot had to be true, it had to be right on the money. Aim for his heart, right in the center of his big, bloated chest. No time to raise the gun and line up the sight. Just point and squeeze all in one motion, hope to hell the slug finds its mark. That fat hombre would shoot me the instant I moved, I knew he would. It would be the last move I'd ever make.

I breathed one last time, a calmness coming over me. Then the man in the ten- gallon hat seemed to go all soft and tender. His knees buckled, and I watched in surprise as he withered, deflating like a giant lawn ornament, coming to rest on the ground in front of me, a feathered shaft in his side. In the rocks, the Indians started singing again – this time not a plainsong but a war cry.

*

When the dust settled, the sky was beginning to lighten. Three men lay face down in the dirt, hog-tied, beside the beaten black horse that had been their ride. The tires looked like pincushions, stuck with arrows, the feather fletching riffling in the wind.

Tonto and I were working to save their lives, the lives of the three men bleeding on the ground. We took care of a tension pneumothorax, a scalped head, and a broken femur, reduced and field-dressed them all nice and tidy. They would live to face trial.

Then, from the back seat, a tremendous fart – an explosion of wind passed in fear. Following the source, we found Bully Ratzer himself, cowering on the floorboard.

"Don't shoot me," he blathered.

We got him outside on the ground, in lithotomy position and hog-tied him with surgical tape for good measure.

"You're finished, Bully Boy," Balmy whispered in his ear as I pulled down his pants, exposing his quivering ass. "I'm exposing you to the world."

The reporter's camera clicked away. "Would you care to comment, Sheriff?"

"Unhand me, you bitches!"

"What most people don't realize is," I nurse-splained in a cheerful, condescending manner, "shit kills. And you, Sheriff Ratzer, are full of shit."

Balmy looked on as I snapped on a pair of gloves and chose the thickest rectal tube in the kit, inserted it into the brown-rimmed anus, inflating the balloon to keep it in place. Next I hooked up the enema bag, filled it with normal saline laced with chili pepper sauce and opened wide the infusion.

"That's what's called a triple-H enema, Balmy. Stands for High, Hot, and Helluvalot.

He cried like a baby, Bully Ratzer did.

On the eastern horizon the sun was a bleeding red gash.

*

The federal marshal had been notified, the Cheyenne medics were en route. The Electricans had taken a wheel off Ratzer's ride and siphoned his gas into my tank; we were ready to roll. I texted Doc Halliday an update. As per instructions, I had delivered the young dancer and saw her reunited with her sister under the protection of the Arapaho. I considered my mission accomplished.

"Good work, Carson," she answered. "The reward of a good deed done is the promise of another one to come. You're not done yet."

What sounded like an eagle's cry pierced the dawn, carrying over the rocks and plains. It was the tribal leader's signal; the warriors leaped to their wheeled ponies and took off, heading north on the highway in a thunderous roar.

Tonto helped me pack up the medical supplies. "Bring Balmy and follow us."

"Where? To the Wind River Reservation?"

He shook his head. "The Arapahos are nomads. We're going to see our cousins, the Sioux. There's a little matter about a pipeline they need our help with."

"Dakota territory? Look, I didn't even bring a change of clothes, I –"

"Hey, can I ride with you too?" Stormy said, getting off the back of Tonto's motorcycle. "That damn seat is killing my ass." The reporter asked to come along too, so he could get his story.

"I'm riding in the back with Mike and his family," said Wyatt. "Abuela's cooking up scrambled eggs, and I'm starving."

"Wait... They've got a kitchen back there?"

"Hot plates," Mike said. "Wired up to your battery."

"We better get charging, then."

The people in the back were no longer invisible, no longer nameless. They were the Trujillos: Angelina, Arturo, Ernesto, and Mike. We were a patchwork family, if only temporarily. We had each other's backs.

While the others jockeyed for their seats in the Power Wagon, Tonto and I embraced behind the sandstone hoodoo. It began as a warm hug of friendship and gratitude, but as I stepped away, he pulled me to him again and kissed me, long and deep, a kiss hot enough to set the prairie on fire.

"Stay with me, Kemosabe," he said in my ear. "We'll figure this out."

I wanted to believe him. Somehow we'd find a way to make the West a good place to live again. Reluctantly we pulled apart, knowing this would continue. This would be consummated. I watched as he swung a leathered leg over the saddle, kick-started his mount and roared off, his long gray braid flying behind him. What the hell are you waiting for,

Carson? I jumped in the cab, threw the Wagon in gear, peeling out in a shower of gravel and dust. Following my conscience, following my heart, following Tonto on the trail to Standing Rock. Drifting up from the back of the truck, the smell of fresh coffee and the sound of voices singing a new day's ballad.

FOUR

MONDAY NIGHT KNIFE & GUN CLUB

Monday night
Calamity
Cough cough bang! Calamity heard it, for reals. The sound woke her up. Something was chasing her. A giant bug was chasing her, Mommy and Wyatt, too. Mommy was coughing and she was shooting at the bug, but it kept on coming, the bullets did not stop it, did not even slow it down. Wide awake now, she covered her mouth to hold back a cough. Mommy! She didn't dare say it out loud. Mommy's at work taking care of sick people, maybe saving their lives, so don't be a baby, Cal, it was only a dream, that's what Wyatt would say. She reached for Dolly, her rag doll, couldn't find her in the tangle of covers. Where was Dolly? Wyatt and Mike, playing in the living room; in her mind's eye she could see their thumbs on the controllers, the cowboys moving across the screen, chasing the bad guys. "Got you, you dirty bastard!" Calamity curled up in a ball beneath the blankets. Keep still. Don't make a sound. But what if that's where the bugs can get you—in your dreams? She hoped Mommy would be OK.

Tonto
Tim Rhodes clipped his I.D. badge onto the pocket of his scrubs.

Tonto RN
www.MyWellmart.com
Like us on Facebook
Follow us on Twitter and Instagram
Healthcare the American Way

There was a barcode to scan for charging meds, dressings, and other supplies. In the bottom right hand corner, his photo. Clean-shaven, hair pulled back in a long braid, a braid once black, now iron gray. Stoic expression.

The whole Emergency staff went by aliases, avatars that represented their personae. Tim had chosen a culturally appropriated, demeaning Hollywood stereotype, embracing it, rebranding it, owning it entirely. The aliases also protected their real names from the public, from patients and vengeful families who might seek retribution or retaliation for some imagined medical misstep. And now the alias also protected him against the Corporate outlaws. More than ever, he was glad for the anonymity.

After scanning his barcode to clock in, Tim took report from the off-going nurse, whose soiled duster and bandanna now lay in a heap in the corner.

"Shit keeps changing," she said, stripping off her gloves. "New orders coming down from Corporate by the hour about who gets treated and how." One thing didn't change, and that was the need for hands-on care. Care and personal protective equipment, which was in short supply.

Tim Rhodes didn't work for the Wellmart Corporation, he worked for the per diem nursing agency. As such, he had the freedom of choosing where and when he worked, and got paid by the hour—almost twice what Wellmart's nurses made—but per diem nurses had no benefits, such as pension, paid vacation, health insurance. Sometimes the work dried up because the hospitals all staffed according to census, and if they could do without a nurse, the corporate bean counters made damn sure they did. But lately there had been plenty of work. Wellmart would have hired him on as one of theirs, but Rhodes didn't want to give up his freedom.

That day, he had worked with the Vigilante Volunteers, making home visits, taking isolated ranch folk coffee and donuts, checking their temperatures and their blood pressures, helping them deliver hay to the cattle still up in the north forty. The flu season had been a bad one. Pneumonia was a lone gunman, picking off the old and the infirm. That metaphor was appropriate for High Plains, where nearly everybody owned a firearm to protect themselves against renegade Indians, outlaws, and crazy in-laws.

In the packed waiting room the poor, tired, huddled masses sat in hard plastic chairs, like third graders waiting for the bell to ring. If they only knew the magic words, Tonto thought. 'Chest pain' or 'Difficulty breathing,' would get you seen quicker. Or if you said nothing because you were unconscious, then you didn't have to wait but were whisked through the double doors to the Treatment Area – Authorized Personnel Only. And, of course, if you came in by ambulance, you got the red-carpet treatment. But a ride in the lifesaving limo, that came with a hefty price. Just last night Sheriff Bully Ratzer had come in by ambulance. He went directly to ICU, he did not pass GO, he did not have to pay $200 out-of-pocket. Sheriff was on the gold-plated health insurance plan; the same one the legislators were on.

Ratzer had himself a bad case of the grippe. The grippe and psychiatric emergencies, they were keeping the nurses busy that spring. Coughers and moon-howlers, they came in droves. The psych cases, the worst ones, were put in the solitary cells at the end of the hall until the psych evaluator on call made it in. Meanwhile, the nurses kept an eye on them, the nurses and the guards. Few ER docs bothered to lay hands on the psych cases. To the compartmentalized Western medicine way of thinking, the head is separate from the body. Insurance companies denied pretty much any claim that originated north of the neckline. Hell, everybody's mind is fucked up to some degree. And so, they denied most psychiatric claims; they had to or they'd be unable to make a profit. Profit, private enterprise, that was the American way. One by one the mental institutions closed, state hospitals shrank by half, and the poor crazies hit the streets with nowhere else to go. Except the emergency department, we take all comers.

Rhodes had been in the healthcare business long enough to know he wasn't going to change how the system operated. Sometimes a cup of kindness is the best medicine. But at Wellmart the nurses were supposed to charge for it; there was a box on the charge sheet they were required to mark if they administered kindness, empathy, or gave a listening ear.

A little after midnight, Tonto managed to break away for a five-minute weather check out on the ambulance ramp. He noticed a change in the wind direction and a halo around the waxing moon. Spring storm was brewing. Cupping his hands against the wind, he lit a cigarette. Heard the deep rumble of a Harley approaching. *Cough cough bang*! But that wasn't a Harley hiccup; Tonto's ear was keen. That bang was a gunshot. He watched as an Indian Chief Dark Horse, a real beauty, like the one Wild Bill used to ride, pulled into the Emergency parking lot, then fell over. Dropping his half-smoked cigarette, he pulled out his phone and punched in a code red before sprinting across the asphalt to where the victim lay, beside his trusty ride.

It *was* Wild Bill. Now, who would want to shoot that old man? One of the rival biker gangs would likely be blamed for the sake of convenience, but Tonto knew better. There's no mistaking the sound of a thirty-caliber Springfield. Not exactly the sort of weapon the motorcycle gangs carried. Pressure on the artery, warm blood still pumping. Bill gasped and gurgled, grabbed Tonto's sleeve and tried to tell him something.

Once they had Wild Bill inside, the team coded him for forty-eight minutes, but it was no use, the old man was a goner. If the bullet hadn't got him, would the grippe have done him in? Or would he have lived many more moons until the chronic obstructive pulmonary disease killed him? Wild Bill was a heavy smoker, but who's to say? You can extend life so long but, in the end, something gets you. The heart fails, the kidneys, or the lungs turn to sponge. The last few weeks of April had seen more deaths than High Plains was accustomed to handling; it was like a big snow-dump of deaths. The old man's friend, that's what they used to call pneumonia. When your life's bills were all mounting, coming due, and it was time to pay the reaper, pneumonia was the one that raised the red flag to the bill collector in black, the guy with the scythe. Pneumonia isn't one specific disease, it's a catch-all term for an infectious process in the lungs. It can be viral or bacterial, it can be caused by inhaling something toxic or by inhaling a bit of food—aspiration pneumonia. This grippe caused pneumonia, it caused the body's immune system to go to war against the little bastards, and sometimes major organs got killed in the crossfire. Collateral damage. 1918 had been a bad year for the grippe, and it had been a bad year for the guys in the trenches shooting at each other across no man's land. Grippe killed more than the war. A similar bug hit us this year. Come spring, it seems to take one last stand, Custer's last stand, determined to go out in a blaze of glory, like a deranged shooter, taking as many with it as it can. Then the snow melts, summer blooms hot and dry, and everybody forgets about the grippe. Until the next bad one hits.

Kit Carson

Monday, my night off. My night to work undercover for the Vigilantes. I showed up at Wellmart in a city slicker suit, pulling a briefcase on wheels, like a pharmaceutical rep. Inside the briefcase, my costume. Thinking, I like the way my spike heels sound, the confident click they make on the linoleum floor. Excited for the card game up in the executive suite. The bigwigs meet up there every Monday night to gamble. Wells Fargo is the House, and they provide a banker to deal cards and handle the accounts. Tonight, Doc Halliday is dealing the cards, though the bigwigs don't know it. They don't know her—she's just an ER doc—and they sure as hell don't know me. They don't know any of us, even though we work right under their noses, on the ground floor beneath them.

On my way in, I saw Olinger's van at the service entrance. Word was, the bodies had been stacking up—in the hospital's cold storage, in the city morgue, in the funeral parlors up and down the Front Range. Crematoriums running day and night, and now that spring thaw had set in, graves were being dug once again.

They say this bug is different and maybe it is. If I seem jaded or blasé, it's just because I've seen a lot of people die from a lot of different causes. And it's never pretty, it's never peaceful, and it's never without collateral damage. No one ever goes gently into that good night, not that I've seen.

*

Tonight, I'm not a nurse, I'm a cocktail waitress for healthcare justice. I'll smile sweet as honey as I lean over the table to hear their order, my cleavage inches from their nose. They don't know the drinks I'll be giving them will be doctored up with MDMA, to help them open up, share their feelings, spill some secrets, show a little compassion, for a change. Maybe see beyond the bottom line.

Until tonight, I'd been keeping my head down, trying to keep food on my table, gas in my Wagon, and the rent paid. Putting in a lot of hours. Nurses are always in demand, but the bean counters don't want to pay for us. The fewer you have to pay, the better. When there's an industrial accident, a train wreck, a mass shooting, or something like that, then you call in the guns for hire—the per diem nurses—like me and Tonto.

A lot had changed in my life, the past few months; the winter had been a hard one. First, the hospital shooting that killed my best friend and shut down the last nonprofit hospital in the West. Then, the whole

Bully Ratzer bullshit went down. Now, the Wether sisters were reunited and working at the casino up in Wind River under new aliases—and under the protection of the Eastern Shoshone and the Northern Arapaho—and the illegals who were living in the back of my truck have moved into my house, but that turned out to be a good thing. Wyatt and Mike are best friends, and the men have jobs, they chip in on the rent. Abuela looks after the kids when I'm at work or volunteering for the Vigilantes, and I come home every day to hot coffee, homemade tortillas, and a pot of green chili on the stove. I've learned to appreciate what's important in life, but there's something missing, something vital, I don't know what.

*

I stepped off the elevator. Wow. So this was where the gods of healthcare lived. Abstract mural on the wall looked like Picasso's Guernica. A tree growing, a real fucking ficus, reaching almost to the skylights. Night watchman at the reception desk, enjoying a cup of coffee. I smiled and held up the fake badge hanging from a lanyard around my neck. Must've looked the part because he smiled back and buzzed me into the executive suite. The double doors opened. I tried not to gawk. Man, this place is tits.

Spied the bar off to the left and ducked in. Shane, dressed smartly in slim black pants and a crisp white shirt, black garters around his sleeves, was playing the role of bartender. In real life, Shane's a nurse anesthetist.

"Where can I change my duds?"

He jerked his thumb over his shoulder, toward a restroom for the staff. I slipped in, opened my briefcase and stripped down, donning the slinky cocktail dress I'd been given to wear. Shook my hair free from the bun, arranging it over my bare shoulders. Then washed my hands in the sink, lathering up with lily-of-the-valley scented soap, taking care to clean under each nail, clipped short, filed smooth, and unvarnished. My hands were not my best feature, but they were clean hands and they were competent.

Shane whistled approvingly when I came out. He was pouring gin into a cocktail shaker.

"Give it to me straight, barkeep. Does this dress make my butt look big?"

"You say that like it's a bad thing."

"Fuck you, Shane." I smiled winsomely. Nothing like a little banter with your colleagues to make the shift bearable.

"How about giving me report? What's the low-down on our patients tonight?" From out in the next room, the conversation grew louder as more players arrived. I had come in cold on this gig and I needed some background info.

"High rollers, every one. See that guy in the white Stetson? That's J.R. Ellsworth, former CEO of Alamo Insurance, headquartered in Dallas. Now he advises the POTUS." J.R.'s diamond bolero sparkled under the track lighting. "Old oil money there", Shane added.

"Next to him, you got Slim Jim Horner, former prosecutor and now territory legislator—eager to make his mark in the political rodeo." Horner, I knew, came from a long line of Esquires and Honorables who had all held political offices of one sort or another.

"On his left there's Billy Palmer Jackson. Looks unpretentious, but don't be fooled—he's a real swingin' dick. Made a fortune in railroads and other investments. I don't know how he figures into this game, but you know what they say?"

"Say about what?"

Shane gave me a patronizing smile. "Follow the money, darlin'. You gotta be rich to be invited to play in this game. Rich and powerful. Now, sitting next to Mr. Jackson is Doctor Hook, CEO of the pharmaceutical company that holds the primary drug concession for Wellmart. Word is, he wants Alamo's contract, but he's up against Johnson & Johnson, and that's Johnson, Jr. next to him, sucking on a platinum toothpick."

I made a mental snapshot of each player and memorized their name, a little trick I had learned taking care of patients. "Whoa, who's the dame?"

"That's Lollie Lovit. I don't know what she does, a hooker or a lobbyist, I'm guessing. Keep your eye on her. She's probably a spotter for one of the big players. And, next to her, that's Little Jim Little, the Lieutenant Governor, and lastly, sitting at the head of the table and licking that big Cubano, that is Big Dick Beamis. Wellmart's head honcho, himself."

"He's shorter than I would've thought."

The top of the CEO's bald head shone pink under the overhead lights. Big Dick Beamis signed our paychecks. Well, not mine because I was a hired gun, I worked for the per diem agency and had no particular loyalty to anyone, except my patients. I collected my earnings, cash on the barrel, the morning after every shift. It was risky business, but I could not find it in myself to commit to Wellmart exclusively.

"So, who are we pulling for, Shane? What's at stake here?" I didn't know much about poker or the business part of healthcare. Hell, all I knew was how to take care of patients, how to carry out doctors' medical orders, how to help people feel better. I knew the ABCs of saving lives, but I didn't have a clue as to how to make a profit from doing so.

"Beamis is a real sumbitch," Shane said. "But he's our sumbitch." He opened a capsule and dropped the powder into a cocktail shaker full of Beefeater. "Molly here should loosen him up. Maybe make him feel a little compassion." He added another capsule, followed by a generous splash of vermouth and a scoop of ice cubes. Then, with a satisfied smile, he put the lid on and shook it lewdly in front of him, just below the level of his belt.

I gave him an eye roll. "You're disgusting."

"What? You want yours stirred?"

"Yeah." I grinned back and held up my freshly washed middle finger, making a slow circle. "Like that."

Shane poured the mixture into chilled martini glasses, added a spear of olives to each one, and placed them on a tray. "Now, git to work, cowgirl." He winked. "And don't forget your mask."

Tonto intercepted him as soon as he came through the door.

"This way," Tonto said, leading the well-dressed young man to one of the psychiatric holding rooms at the end of the hall. It was the card dealer from the house bank, Wells Fargo. He carried a briefcase with the outline of a stagecoach drawn by three horses embossed into the rich brown leather.

"But I'm not here for treatment," the man insisted. "I'm here on business. Important business."

"Standard procedure and recommended precaution," Tonto said, in a quiet but firm voice, a voice that could calm a rattling snake and convince it to slither away. "Just a routine temperature scan." The banker complied, and Ruth Halliday followed them into the room.

"Have you been out of the territory recently? Been exposed to anyone with the grippe? Exhibiting flu-like symptoms?" Tonto ran a digital thermometer across the banker's forehead.

"None of this is necessary, I assure you. The boss is expecting me upstairs."

Tonto pressed his lips together. Showed the reading to Halliday. She cocked an eyebrow with exaggerated drama, said, "Mister, I'm afraid your body temperature is abnormal. You'll need to strip down to your skivvies; we have to collect a specimen. A stool sample." That wasn't quite true; she needed his costume for a few hours. Not to mention they had run out of grippe testing kits hours ago.

"But I feel fine,"

"That's what they all say, at first. But we can't take any chances. I'll step outside, the nurse here will assist you. Oh, and I'll need to decontaminate your briefcase."

"But—"

"Standard procedure. Don't worry, you'll get it back."

Halliday left Tonto to attend to the Wells Fargo employee. The plan was to keep him locked up in the psychiatric isolation room until the card game was over. Well, at least he'd be safe in there.

*

They were running out of medical supplies, out here on the frontier. Good citizens were sewing masks from fabric scraps, God bless them, and it helped slow down the onslaught. One bug, one single virus, a packet of genes, can't kill you but an army of them can. Ruth was philosophical when it came to death. For her, life and death was a game. Death for the individual is a given, the House always wins, but when and how you die, now that's the interesting part. In some games, you can buy time, but at what price? Medicine is a numbers game, dodging stats and likely outcomes, outsmarting standard deviations, becoming an outlier on the right side of the curve. You know your odds, but still you take your chances, you play the hand you've been dealt. It's the playing that matters. There is no winning, there is only the playing. Life is a card game and death is the lone gunman who comes to collect.

Just that evening, she had seen him in the parking lot, three, maybe four, cars away. A tall figure, dressed in a long black duster and carrying a bolt action rifle. The old pit boss himself. And then he was gone—ducked down between the cars or vanished into thin air. He had let himself be seen on purpose, and Ruth Halliday was glad for the reminder. Seeing him close at hand always made her feel more alive.

Now dressed in the dealer's confiscated clothes, she felt a rush of excitement, the very act of disguise, an aphrodisiac. Crisp white linen shirt, black sleeve garters, silk bowtie, and a richly brocaded vest. Close-cropped hair greased smooth, and a paste-on 'stache under her black silk bandanna. Inside the Wells Fargo briefcase, her own deck of cards. Halliday was a tough old buffalo soldier, a medic in the wars before she became an Emergency Medicine physician. According to some, the best practitioner in High Plains, before Insurance companies took control. But the doctor's real passion was Blackjack. Blackjack and cosplay.

*

The corporate den was abuzz with conversation when she entered, using the dealer's access badge. The old military training came back as she automatically appraised the room in a shrewd sweeping glance, sizing up the players, making a mental map of the space, ingress and egress, identifying possible hiding places. She saw Kit, their eyes met briefly, casually, as the nurse flirted with the Suits, offering them drinks, doing the form-fitting, low-cut cocktail waitress outfit justice. They were used to working together in the ER, digging out bullets, impactions, treating-and-streeting ‘em or sending them to the floor. Working with a good nurse was like dancing with a good partner, no convo needed. Halliday had handpicked Kit as her protégé, saw her potential as a partner. With a little training, that one would be an excellent card player. Like the best nurses, Carson was a keen observer of detail with a sixth sense for subclinical symptoms. She was new to cards, she didn’t know all the rules and ramifications, but that nurse definitely had the instincts. The two of them, working a casino together, now that was pleasurable to think about. But first, to get through this night with some sort of advantage for the Vigilantes and the people of High Plains.

She stepped into the center of the gaming table with the confidence of stepping up to the bedside of a patient in full cardiac arrest. Alert, scrubbed, gloved, and masked. Eight players already seated in the oversized, overstuffed, leather chairs; on their phones, placing other wagers, in other games, countless deals going on all over the West. No masks or gloves for them. Let the little people halt the spread of grippe, the crème of High Plains couldn’t be bothered. She cleared her throat, the sign for them to finish their transactions. Waited until they pocketed their phones, knowing she had ‘em where she wanted ‘em. Having researched their backgrounds thoroughly, she knew their salaries and their CVs, their medical histories, she knew who was premenstrual, perimenopausal, and who had erectile dysfunction. She knew what was at stake at this table tonight—the access to healthcare in High Plains. Picking up a deck in her dexterous hands—hands skilled at palpating, percussing, suturing, and sleight of hand—she shuffled the deck and went to work. Read ‘em and weep.

Throwing a card game was not a sure thing. Most of the players, Halliday noticed, were playing dry and sober; their doctored drinks sat untouched in front of them, the ice melting. Lollie Lovit was a spotter; she gave herself away with her unnecessary movements, touching her ear, twirling her hair. These Monday night card games were more than good old boy camaraderie, way more. It wouldn’t devolve into a corporate rave, which would have been easier to take advantage of, but Ruth Halliday, that old ace in the hole, knew more than one way to manipulate a game. She had her eye on a stockpile of valuable medical equipment and PPE needed right here in High Plains. If Big Dick Beamis played his cards right, those supplies would be his to control.

Kit

Another hand played, and if I understood it right, Wellmart's health insurance just changed to Alamo. Whether this was good or bad I couldn't say, but probably bad. There hadn't been an increase in nurses' benefits since the year the unions were run out of town. Things weren't going according to plan. The players weren't drinking anything but bottled water, the good stuff, from Italy and France. The martinis laced with molly sat untouched on the table, and instead of loosening up and growing more empathetic and loving, the players were becoming more withdrawn, getting harder to read. I was trying to learn all I could—about the game, about the stakes, about the personalities of these high rollers—by watching their plays, their body language, and reading their faces.

Big Dick started sweating profusely. He was trying hard to maintain his poker face, a face darkening from pink to purple. He looked like he could use some more water, so I brought him a fresh bottle, opened it there at the table. But something was wrong. What was it? He seemed frozen, yet there was panic in his eyes. Was he choking?

"Can I get you something else, Mr. Beamis? Mr. Beamis, are you OK?" Oh shit, oh hell, he was definitely not OK. "Can you speak? Are you choking?"

Halliday shot me a reprimanding scowl; it was out of line to talk to the players. If they wanted something, they would signal me. But I didn't care about poker etiquette; I was trying to save a life. I bent down, put my hand on his chest, felt it rise and fall. Felt his breath hot on my face. Not choking, his airway was patent. "Mr. Beamis, can you smile? Give me a smile now, will you?" I was all up in his face now, assessing his expression, looking for symmetry. This was no poker face, this was a half-paralyzed face. "Stick your tongue out, let's see some tongue." But though the left side of his face twitched, he could not do it.

The other players stared mutely, shocked at my intrusion. For a moment there was no other sound in the room but the icemaker in the bar, rattling with a new delivery of cubes. Then Halliday's stern voice, reprimanding me for interrupting the game. She was a doctor, did she not see this man was stroking out? The cards in his right hand fell to the floor. I saw a jack and a queen of diamonds face up on the hardwood. Still, the others maintained their poker faces. Did they not see? Or were they too scared to react?

"Squeeze my hands, Mr. Beamis. Squeeze as hard as you can." His left hand squeezed mine, but his right hand was lifeless. Reached for my phone, but dammit, there wasn't a pocket to be had in this ridiculously tight dress. Remembered I left my phone on the bar. "Somebody call Emergency," I said. But no one moved. "Shane!" I looked toward the adjoining room, saw him sitting at the bar chowing down on Chinese take-out, his earbuds in. I hurried over, grabbed my phone and called the Emergency Department my own damn self.

"Kate, is that you? This is Kit Carson. Send a team up to the corporate suite, asap. I've got a middle-aged white male with an acute onset of right-sided hemiparesis. The victim is conscious, but unable to speak. Stroke protocol. Call EKG, radiology, pharmacy."

"Corporate suite? Where the hell is that?"

"Five floors above you. Use your tracking device. I'll leave my phone on."

Beamis needed intravenous access and tPA to dissolve the clot. He needed blood pressure intervention and continuous monitoring; he needed an anticonvulsant. He needed a CT scan, or better yet, an MRI. Halliday knew it, Shane knew it. Was I the only one who saw what was happening? Were my colleagues too much into their alter-egos to recognize and respond appropriately? I stood by the stricken man, talking to him, my hand on his shoulder, reassuring him, and in three minutes flat the ER team had come up and rolled him away, but there was no making up for the fact that Wellmart's CEO had folded, and those stockpiled supplies we needed were not in his possession.

"Is he gonna make it?" Lollie Lovit asked, the only one who said anything. The other players looked down at their hands, not wanting to show any emotion, not while the game was in play. After all, Beamis's misfortune was none of their own. Halliday finished the round, distributed the chits, then the players got up and left. I wondered if anyone had called his wife.

Shane collected all the spiked martinis, pouring them into a gallon jug. “Can’t let this stuff go to waste. Call your friends, Kit, we’ll make our own little party.”

I smiled and shook my head no. “Sorry, Shane. All I want is to change out of this sleazy dress and go home to my kids.” Calamity had texted me about a bad dream she had. She needed her mother and I needed a good night’s sleep.

But a good night’s sleep was not in the cards for me. We had to get our hands on those medical supplies before they were all loaded onto Billy Jackson Palmer’s freight train and hauled away.

“Kit, we need you and your wagon,” Halliday said. “Meet Tonto downstairs and get going.”

Tonto

Meanwhile, down in the Emergency Department, Tim Rhodes had given the Wells Fargo dealer a thorough assessment, holding him until the card game was over, performing a traditional Arapaho prayer dance for his benefit before releasing the bewildered hostage with complimentary samples of antihistamine.

The man called Tonto felt his practice to be a pastiche of traditions and beliefs. He was a man of science, practiced modern medicine, yet he smoked tobacco on occasion, and marijuana to relax; he burned sage to purify the air, he fasted and ingested peyote for visions of clarity. The man called Tonto had built his own sweat lodge, and he sang Arapaho prayers, yet he had seen firsthand the value of third generation antibiotics, genetic testing and computerized tomography scans. He also knew there were no certain cures for any disease; a man’s will to live or his wish to die could not be discounted. The man called Tonto was a white man’s nurse and an Arapaho healer. He was a medicine man.

The older he got the more he felt an affinity for the old ways. He belonged to a time when his people hunted elk and bison with bow and arrow, ate the meat, the organs, used the bone and horn for tools, wrapped themselves in the hide. Animals and plants were sacred because they were alive, they sustained life, they made life possible. On the other hand, he had never once ridden a flesh-and-blood horse; but he was at one with his two-wheeled steel horse. Unlike most people of High Plains, he did not carry a gun. Yet he had killed a man with his bow and arrow. He had killed protecting others not of his tribe.

*

In anticipation of the raid on the Fort, Tonto called on his brothers, the Arapahos and the Cheyenne, and the Old White Guys on Wheels, those bikers who collected toys for kids at Christmas and held summer rides to raise money for warriors wounded in battle. They would do it, they would all unite for a just cause, healthcare for all.

Even while the game was going on five stories above him, Tonto had done his research on the internet, in the palm of his hand. The Fort was being used as a supply depot again, just as it once had been back in the 1860's when the U.S. government stockpiled annuities for the Indians there. The annuities—grain and other food, tools, hardware—were given in accordance to the Treaty of Fort Wise, a dubious agreement which reduced the size of the reservation the Cheyenne and Arapaho had been granted under the previous Treaty of Fort Laramie, which had been broken by the whites when gold was discovered in Colorado.

A little recon in the field by the Cheyenne named Lone Tree had determined that the supplies were already loaded into a shipping container and waiting for pick-up in the parking lot. There would be security to deal with—a locked gate, security lights, cameras, silent alarms. The trick was to get in and out quick. Tonto assigned three of his brothers to help him load. Kit would stay behind the wheel, the wagon in the get-away position.

Kit

Riding shotgun beside me, Tonto, his cell phone on speaker. He was coordinating with the bikers. We were about ten minutes out. According to Plan A, we'd load up my wagon, and then we'd be outta there in a hurry. Get in, get out, and nobody gets hurt. We hoped to have the element of surprise working for us. Tonto and me, we made quite a team, and I was proud the Vigilantes chose me to accompany him. Did Halliday know what a good team we were? Or maybe it was just my wagon they needed. I didn't care. With Tonto riding shotgun, I could've robbed a bank. Me and Tonto, Belle Starr and Jesse James. Come summer, when all of this was past, I was looking forward to holing up somewhere with Tonto, just the two of us, for a long weekend together.

A pair of bolt cutters severed the chain that held the gate closed. The bikers entered and formed a circle around the block of containers in the lot, waiting to be picked up. One of the bikers cut the lock on one of the doors, someone shined a flashlight inside. What the hell—coffins? We went to the next container, same thing. Every container stacked high with them. Instead of masks, gloves, and paper gowns, we've got caskets. Instead of lifesaving gear and equipment, we've got fucking pine boxes.

"Look at this," Tonto said, shining the flashlight down at our feet. Fresh tire tracks in the spring mud and a large rectangle of dry ground where another container had been.

Our lifesaving supplies had been picked up before we got there and were probably headed for the train depot. With a war cry, Tonto alerted his riders who roared off to intercept them.

*

It hit me like an iron horse. The crushing fatigue, the fire in my joints, burning eyes, the aching in my head. Shivering, I leaned against the hood of my wagon, warm from the ride, absorbing its heat.

"Don't come too close," I warned. "Keep your distance. I've been hit."

"You've been shot?"

"No, it's the grippe, the bug, I've got it. I feel like hell."

"If you've got it, I've already been exposed," Tonto said. "Give me the keys. I'll drive us out of here."

He opened the door, he helped me into the passenger seat where I collapsed, like a marionette whose strings have been cut. Just to breathe was a supreme effort. One at a time, like climbing a mountain. Tonto at the wheel, his duster over me, a faint smell of buffalo hide, sage, and cigarette smoke, the motion of the wagon vibrating my bones, my dry and thirsty bones. Where are we going? I don't care, just keep moving, keep moving, my throat's burned dry and my soul does cry for water. Cool, clear water. Sing that song for me, would you?

Outside the window, drawing up beside us in the next lane, a white hearse, pale in the starlight. I couldn't see the driver through the tinted window, but I knew he was coming for me. The lone gunman, putting down victims one by one. Was it murder? Justifiable homicide? Or was it mercy killing? They put down dogs, don't they? Our beloved four-legged friends. But I can't die. I've got responsibilities. Who will raise my children? Long minutes passed, or was it hours, maybe days, and it occurred to me that they were already grown, Wyatt and Calamity Jane, grown and long gone, and I had missed it. But maybe it wasn't too late. Tonto was still driving, he would protect me, he was both warrior and medicine man. We were hurtling through the night at the speed of light, we were bound for some distant ranch, or a sweat lodge. That I would die, that was a fact. I had died before, many times, and now it was time to die again. Oh, the mystery, the pain, the wonder and the why of it all.

They say the sense of hearing is the last to go and the first to come back. When at last the fever broke and the coughing began, I woke to noise. Disembodied voices, the buzz and hum of medical equipment, the incessant beep, a nagging reminder that somewhere, someone's IV needed attention. I recognized the masked figures caring for me, not by name but by profession. Nurses, they knew what to do. A nurse had my back. The lone gunman was nowhere in sight, but if he came for me, if he had a bullet with my name on it, the nurse would listen like a priest, accept my shortcomings and grant me my last request. A nurse would ease my pain, brush my hair, bring my children to say goodbye.

This bug, you can't kill it with a bullet. The body can fight it but, in the end, it's up to the lone gunman whether I live or die. With any luck and a lot of science, there will be a vaccine, but sure as shootin' a new bug will come along. There is no place left to hide, not even in your dreams.

I am a child again, riding in the back seat of the buckboard half asleep or half awake, the vibration relaxing me, loosening my thoughts, jiggling them away from my brittle joints, freeing my soul. Cholera hit the wagon train, killed so many of us that year. Killed the natives too, like the smallpox and the diphtheria. Killed more than bullets, these bugs. Still, the nurse cared for me.

If I die, let it be a burning revelation, a cool drink of relief, a glorious reward. Death, the lone gunman, an afternoon nap, a morning dream, a morphine dream. I'm dreaming I'm playing poker at the big golden table and I'm there, standing in line to be born, waiting to be dealt my card, a luckier card this time.

Calamity

It had only been five days since she had last seen her mother in person, felt her strong hands comb the tangles from her hair, making her eyes sting, before parting it in a straight line on her scalp and making two braids down her back. She liked it when mommy fixed her hair, even though it hurt a little bit. Today, she had finally let Abuela brush and braid her hair, but it didn't feel quite the same when she did it. Even when mommy was at work, all night long, she knew she was helping people, that was her job. Now, the bug had got her mother and the other nurses were taking care of her. But she should be all better by now. Mommy was strong and Calamity wanted her.

"Wyatt, when is mommy coming home?"

Her brother's eyes never left the screen, his thumbs furiously working the controller, trying his best to stay alive, and to kill the last bad guy left standing. If he knew, he wasn't saying.

FIVE

TUESDAY NIGHT REQUIEM

Tuesday afternoon

In a rented room at the 4Aces, a seen-better-days motel that sheltered East Colfax drifters, drovers, and drug addicts, the man who called himself the Lone Gunman stood before the bathroom mirror, armed with a toothbrush. His mama had always urged him to take care of his teeth. *Brush and floss religiously, Willie. Take good care of your teeth, and don't take up smoking, methamphetamines or cocaine, you'll ruin those pearly whites.* His beloved mama, God rest her soul, had been a dental assistant, the best damn dental hygienist in High Plains. She had also urged him to be a good boy Willie, and never play with guns. He took that advice very seriously; he never *played* with guns; he took them very seriously. Guns were his livelihood, and today he was going to make a killing.

After a final rinse and spit, Willie wiped his mouth with the white terrycloth motel towel and admired his reflection. His lean cheeks and square jawline sported a two-day growth of salt-and-pepper hair – the stubble was a desirable look for High Plains cowboys. He lifted the black silk bandanna so that it rested across the bridge of his nose, covering his lower face and neck. Adjusting the brim of the black felt cowboy hat forward so that it hid his receding hairline and cast a shadow over his eyes, he scrutinized his image. Yepper, a fair enough facsimile.

He wasn't the real Lone Gunman, that myth, that legend, that Western metaphor for Death, but he had cultivated a true aim and abandoned his conscience somewhere along the trail, traits he thought suited him for the job. Like the Grim Reaper himself, the Lone Gunman was feared yet ignored. Folks didn't talk about the Lone Gunman; it was better to pretend you didn't see him standing there alone, all hangdog off to the side, like a boy at a square dance without a partner.

The way Willie saw it, the Lone Gunman was Death's own angel. Tonight, his target, the sick nurse named Kit Carson, would go to her just reward. She'd probably thank him, if she could. And he would be well compensated for it. But even when he didn't have a paying job, the Lone Gunman kept his skills honed by picking off the old and the weak, lungers and coughers who spread their germs and sucked in more than their share of the allocated breath of life. Looking at it scientifically, he filled an ecological niche. Back before antibiotics were developed, pneumonia was deemed "the old man's friend." Inflammation of the lungs took old folks after a bout of the grippe or a fall and a broken hip. It finished them off, humanely, some would say. Pneumonia could be a blessing in disguise for those who had reached the end of their skein of existence. People clamored for "life support," not realizing they were already receiving life support – the best modern science had to offer. Today there were cures and vaccines for every damn little thing. There was no rest for the weary.

The way he saw it, what he did, he did in the name of love. There, by the door, his chosen instrument – a bolt action Springfield .30-06 – fine piece of Americana. His heirloom was in immaculate condition – cleaned, oiled, rubbed to a sheen and ready to do the master's bidding. None of those automatic slaughter machines for him. They were for pussies who shot up schools and shopping malls. The Lone Gunman had a reputation for selectivity. With his precision, his steady hand, he might have been a sniper or a surgeon. With his passion, his keen perception, his sense of timing, he might have been an artist or a musician.

The merciful assassin checked his pocket watch. The mission

depended on precise timing; he needed to enter the facility during the change of shift. A tingling in his blood. It was time.

One last glance in the mirror. He pulled down the bandanna and drew back his lips in a skeletal, rictus grin – his teeth, big, white, and even as a picket fence. American teeth. Mama would be proud. He would bequeath them to the High Plains Dental Institute in her honor. The image of his own grinning skull mounted on the wall like a trophy, the image gave him a comforting sense of immortality.

Wyatt

"Wyatt, are we going to have a funeral?" His little sister, breaking through the soundproof booth inside his mind. The boy's heart froze. *She knew.* His tongue lay heavy in his mouth. Someone had told her, she guessed it, or maybe she dreamt it. Calamity was always talking about her dreams.

"Are we, Wyatt?"

He could not think of what to say. He could not even think about it, much less speak of it. "Stop talking so much; I'm trying to concentrate." His thumbs moved like lightning across the buttons of the controller.

"But we have to have a funeral. Abuela found my poor dead Hammie in the freezer, inside your sock, and she was going to put him in the trash, but I said no because Mommy said we would bury Hammie under the cottonwood trees in the summertime, after a rainstorm, when the ground is soft. Mommy promised we'd have a funeral, a celebration of his life. She said I could pad a shoebox with cottonwood seeds and sing Happy Trails. She said I could borrow her black bandanna for a pall. What's a pall, Wyatt?

He shrugged. "Ask Abuela."

"OK, but we have to wait for Mommy to get well and come back home. We can't have a funeral without Mommy."

"Sure, we'll wait for her." He felt a breath of relief rush out of his body. This was all about the fucking hamster that had died months ago. If Calamity believed Mom was going to get well, maybe there was still hope. He wanted to believe but dared not, lest he be crushed. He wanted to save her. There must be something he could do. But what?

Onscreen, his avatar took a direct hit and disappeared in a puff of simulated smoke.

The video game no longer gave him pleasure. He was fidgety, like a bronc in a holding pen. It wasn't only his mother's illness that made him restless; there was something else, a feeling that he was missing out on his own life, held captive inside this crowded house. Stay inside, Wyatt. It's dangerous out there. Stay inside, stay safe. Well, he didn't want to stay inside anymore, and he didn't want to stay safe. He wanted to venture out, take a risk, do something different, maybe even dangerous. Something to make his blood race. It seemed to Wyatt that he had spent too much of his life indoors, surrounded by walls, by rules, protected. Mom had always warned him about the bad people out there. *Lock the door, don't answer it, do your homework, watch your sister*. Meanwhile, Mom went out and did battle with the world, night after night, and look what that got her--it got her sick, maybe even killed. Now it was his turn. He was old enough to have some hair on his balls. That made him a man, right? Or very nearly so. And what was he going to do with his life? Be a video game champion? No, that was just killing time. Practice. For the real thing, which Old Man Henderson next door always said was coming.

Later that afternoon…

"Come on, Mike. Let's go."

"Where to, Wyatt?"

"Downtown. Balmy's on the Three-Ten to High Plains. You want to come along?"

"Sure."

An adventure was no good if it wasn't shared. His best friend, Mike Trujillo, was his only friend. A whole year younger than Wyatt, Mike knew so much more about High Plains street life, having lived in homeless camps for some months before his family took shelter in the back of Kit's truck and soon after found their way inside the Carson's home. Now, having escaped the boring confines of the house, they were on a mission; they were going to the Trailways station to meet Balmy, who was on her way down from Indian Country where she had been hiding out with sister Stormy under the protection of the Arapaho and the Shoshone.

Wyatt took a handful of coins from the Mason jar on his mother's dresser. He thought about taking the Glock from under his bed, but the piece was too big. Too obvious. Besides, it was the house weapon -- meant to kill home intruders and for that reason should stay in the home. Instead, he chose the Smith & Wesson seven-shooter, an antique pocket pistol from the family heirloom case, and loaded it with the accompanying .22 black powder cartridges. Fact: Samuel Clemens had carried one of these on his travels out West, he bragged to Mike. Yeah, Mark fucking Twain. It doesn't get more American than that.

"Do you really want to walk around with a loaded antique gun in your pants pocket?" Personally, Mike preferred to carry a folding knife his uncle had given him.

But Wyatt had read Samuel Clemens's article "Advice to Youth" in which the great writer warns of the danger of unloaded firearms. Said the wag, *They are the most deadly and unerring things that have ever been created by man. You don't have to have any sights on the gun, you don't have to take aim, even. No, you just pick out a relative and bang away, and you are sure to get him. A youth who can't hit a cathedral at thirty yards with a Gatling gun in three-quarters of an hour, can take up an old empty musket and bag his mother every time at a hundred.*

The irony and sarcasm went over Wyatt's juvenile head. His heart pounded, but not with fear. Not exactly. It felt more like excitement. And what was the difference between fear and excitement? He aimed to find out.

The two boys walked through the neighborhoods – Mexican, Italian, Hungarian – cutting through the alleyways toward the bottomland where the tracks ran, where the small population of Chinese had set up their laundries, their restaurants, their drug dens, right alongside the poorer sort of billiard rooms, brothels, and Irish grog shops. Red paper lanterns hanging over the street, there seemed to be some kind of festival going on – vendors selling white dumplings from street carts and the pop- pop of firecrackers in the allies. Gang tags everywhere. Waddies, Toros, Tongs, Latin Kings. Mike knew which group had made which signs, or at least he claimed to know. "We don't want to be here after dark, Wyatt."

Wyatt was aware of the weapon, felt it solid against his thigh with every step. They bought two bottles of Fanta at an immigrant convenience store, guzzled them down in the shade cast on the east side of the building. Late afternoon, still hot, it would stay light a long, long time. Summer days were endless.

A man lying on the sidewalk, next to a buggy piled high with supplies. Was he sleeping, or was he dead? People walked right past him, like he wasn't even there. Wyatt guessed he was passed out drunk or overdosed. Should he call for help? Why wasn't anyone else doing anything? He knew what his mother would do. Wyatt touched 9-1-1 on his keypad.

"There's a man down on the sidewalk, Fifteenth and Wazee. I don't know what's wrong. I think he might need some help."

Minutes later, flashing lights. Wyatt wanted to stay and watch but the lawman said, "You kids run along. Git on home, go on." Mike pulled at his sleeve, anxious to keep moving. The Law made him nervous.

Hearing the crack of pool balls, they stopped at a basement saloon, beneath the Oriental Palace: Poolhall, Saloon and Chinese Take-Out, the sign advertised. Six feet under the main floor of the hotel, cool and dark as a grave, lit only by flickering neon beer signs. The clink of glasses, the easy talk of men. A whiff of whiskey and a hint of sewer gas. Wyatt watched the men rack 'em up three times, watching carefully, seeing how the game was played. A Chinese kid, a boy about Wyatt's own age; it was hard to tell. Name of Zhang. Said he worked there. Ran errands for customers, delivered food, pushed a broom, and brushed the felt tops of the billiard tables. Wyatt envied him his freedom. Working meant money and money meant freedom. At least to Wyatt it did.

"Want to play?"

"Does it cost money?"

Zhang grinned. "Depends."

"On what?"

"On whether you win or lose."

"I don't have any money."

"Do you have anything to put up? Anything of value?

Wyatt felt the weight of the pistol deep in his pocket.

"Yeah."

"Let's see it."

He withdrew the antique revolver, opening his fingers to reveal it, like a choice crabapple.

Zhang nodded approvingly. "That's a nice little piece. Does it actually fire?"

"I wouldn't carry it if it didn't. And yeah, it's loaded." But he wasn't certain if it would actually fire, the black powder cartridges were so old.

"What do you have to put up, Zhang?" Mike, looking after his friend's interest.

"Joss."

"What's that?"

"It's money. Not the kind you spend here on Earth."

"Who wants that?"

"The ghosts of our ancestors."

Wyatt laughed. "How can they spend it if they're dead? You can't take it with you."

Zhang shrugged. "Maybe you can. We burn it for them, and it goes up in smoke."

Wyatt felt a breath of cold air touch the back of his neck. "Well, I don't believe in ghosts. What else you got?"

Zhang chewed his lip as he considered the question, then pulled a plastic bag out of his pocket. It held a wad of something gray, maybe some kind of drug, or maybe it was a rhino's balls, or some weird Chinese herb. Wyatt didn't want to reveal his ignorance.

"I changed my mind. I don't want to put up my piece."

"Then you shouldn't have pulled it out of your pants, cowboy." Zhang grinned, breaking the tension. "Hey, look, I'll play you cowboys one game, just for the hell of it. No bets. But next time, bring silver, OK? More fun that way." He handed them cue sticks from the rack on the wall and a cube of chalk from his pocket. The boys chalked the tips of their sticks as they had seen the other players do.

"Go ahead. You break 'em," Zhang said.

Wyatt racked the balls, then placed the cue ball where the others had, carefully lining up his shot. Just then his cell phone pinged with an incoming text. It was Balmy, at the station. Shooting pool would have to wait.

Balmy Wether

Moms real sick, maybe dyin, I thought you should know.

Reading Wyatt's text, her gut twisted, and she had answered impulsively.

Im on my way.

It was dangerous, but Balmy had been planning to go back to High Plains anyway, to meet with Polly Pry, the outlaw reporter from the Rocky Mountain Gazette. Starr had brought down more than one political career since coming to the territory. The last reporter, the back-east dude who interviewed Stormy after the shootout on the border of Wyoming, that reporter had been fired, or maybe even shot. In any case, the story had been killed, that much was apparent. Buried somewhere deep in the back pages with the unimportant news, the happenings no one ever read, or shared, or tweeted, or gave a shit about. Ratzer's campaign posse probably saw to that.

But Balmy Wether had yet to tell her own story, a bigger story than the breach of some two-bit nondisclosure agreement between a pole dancer and a political pimp. She had been following Polly Pry on social media. Now she messaged her and arranged a meeting to expose Bully Ratzer. The timing was perfect, with the election only a few months away. This time the story would not be killed; she would see to that. And now going to High Plains was even more imperative. Nurse Kit Carson was real sick, Wyatt had said.

The next day, Balmy was at the bus stop in Riverton, ticket in hand, purchased with the money she made waiting tables at the café. Dressed in baggy, secondhand sweats and cheap running shoes, she thought she might pass for a boy. Her scalp stung from a dozen nicks and cuts. She had shaved her own head so she wouldn't be recognized by Ratzer's men, who were everywhere in High Plains. Balmy's long dark hair, arrow straight and shiny as a crow's feather, had been a hallmark of hers when she danced. Hair down to the bottom of her butt. Now that it was shaved off, she felt light. Much cooler. Less burdened. Stronger, somehow. It felt like the opposite of Samson, was it Samson? Samson and Delilah, yeah. Balmy's hair had been her weakness, and now that she had cut it off, she felt liberated. Her hair was history – she had been released from her past.

Traveling light, all she owned in a pillowcase. Everyone else on the motor coach was packing heat, but all she had for a weapon was a pointed nail file. And no hair to hide behind. At least she did have a smartphone. Information was power, information could be used as a weapon, although it was slower than a bullet or the thrust of a knife. Unlike bullets, information was unlimited, with a smartphone or a computer you would never run out. She was still unsure about which information was reliable and which was bullshit, but she was learning. Having just earned her G.E.D. online, Balmy had enrolled in online classes at Arapaho Community College. She wanted to be a journalist. She wanted to expose all the injustice in the world, starting with Sheriff Bully Ratzer.

Now that Stormy was safe with the Indians, working at the casino under a new name, Balmy could get on with her life. She had never wanted to be a sex worker. What young girl dreams of being a lap dancer when she grows up? Unlike Stormy, who claimed her great-great grandmother was full blooded Shoshone, Balmy could prove no tribal affiliation. In truth, she didn't know who she was or where she had come from. She had blended genetic traits, being the eye-pleasing product of mixed-race parentage, a slightly exotic look, with dark, wideset eyes and a dusky hue to her flawless skin. But her past was a blank slate. She had no memories of a mother, much less a father. No roots to ground her. Balmy was a free bird. And that called for a new name. She was no longer half of the Stormy and Balmy Wether Sisters act. Stormy might have signed a nondisclosure with Ratzer but Balmy hadn't. At fifteen, she hadn't been old enough to sign a legal document. She still wasn't "legal" in that sense, which made Ratzer's crime all the worse. Sex trafficking of minors. It was bad enough he was a crooked sheriff, abusing his position, making money from criminal activities, but she hated herself for having done his bidding. There was no amount of money that would take that shame away. She would expose him, she would bring him down, she would end his political aspirations and, in the process, kick-start her own career in investigative journalism.

But poor Wyatt and sweet little Calamity. Balmy's heart tightened thinking about them. She felt a duty to help them and to help Kit, the nurse who had risked her life for her and sheltered her after what happened to Stormy.

The Trailways coach slowed as it prepared to pull into the station. Her phone said 3:10. She texted Polly Pry, *Arrived.* The reporter texted back, *Meet me at the Oriental*.

Looking up from her phone, Balmy caught a glimpse of a black town car with tinted windows parked across the street. Nervous, she ran a hand across her bare head. *Relax. Could be any pimp's ride*. As the bus braked to its final stop, she fired off a text to Tonto to let him know of her arrival. She would need some backup. Especially when the dirt she had on Ratzer hit the wind.

Tonto

When he received Balmy's text, Tim Rhodes had just activated his phone after three days of being off the grid. Immediately, the screen filled with urgent messages.

The man known as Tonto was on his way back from the Arapaho Sundance, having gone to find an herb, a berry, a bark, a root – some authentic healing concoction or decoction, something to cure Kit, to rid her of the grippe. And peyote, he had gone for that too. For the insight, the greater vision, it might bring. He regretted having waited so long in life to embrace his Arapaho blood. Western medicine was failing him, it was failing everyone. The scientific process was being subverted by profit, by corporate greed. The basis of Western Medicine was science based, and the basis of Western hospitals was professional nursing care, and both had been subverted. The answer, his answer, was to start a non-profit hospital owned and operated by nurses. A co-op organization, like a credit union.

Tonto stopped just north of Fort Collins to relieve himself and to reconnect with the wider world. Turned his cellphone on and discovered the shit had hit the fan again. Wellmart was in chaos. Patients' lives were in danger, including Kit's – not just from the bug but from lack of medical attention and skilled nursing care. The corporate bottom line was killing people and on top of that, Balmy Wether had left the reservation, was back in High Plains, Ratzer's goons were hell-bent on silencing his opposition and the so-called Lone Gunman was still at large, delivering deadly bullets in a random sort of fashion. Or maybe they were working together. And all he wanted to do was to start a nonprofit hospital, then retire. He was ready to enjoy the good life. Hunting, fishing, riding. Drinking a beer or smoking a joint and watching the sun go down. Watching his grandkids grow up. Which seemed unlikely, since to his knowledge, he had not fathered any children. But there were always surrogates. Blood wasn't everything. Kit had children in need of a father figure.

Richard 'Big Dick' Beamis

Help! Nurse!

He tried to make the words come out of his mouth, but they got lost somewhere in the uncharted territory of his brain. *Where in this hell was his nurse?*

Richard Beamis, the chief executive officer of Wellmart Healthcare Corporation, was a VIP patient in his own hospital's Intensive Care Unit. He had been there a week with little change in his critical, but stable, condition. There were no moves being made to transfer him home or to rehab, or even to the neuro floor. It was an awkward situation. Beamis was taking up valuable real estate – the ICU was for those who needed high level nursing care and monitoring, and the miracles of modern life support that the ICU nurses and respiratory therapists knew how to operate. They worked as a specially trained force, like the Navy SEALS, they were SWAT Nurses. As the hospital's head honcho, Beamis deserved the level of staffing available only in this elite unit. The physicians were reluctant to move him anywhere, despite pressure from the insurance company. The ailing CEO of Wellmart deserved the very best the company had to offer.

Even though the hospital ran well enough on its own, Beamis was the self-styled visionary who drove the corporation's policy of growth and acquisition, that, in turn, fueled the confidence in the market. Healthcare was big business in America, presenting limitless opportunities for growth. After all, everyone was born and everyone needed interventions throughout their lives, and in the end, everyone died. From cradle to grave, every intervention could be provided by Wellmart, the largest for-profit healthcare company in the American West. But Richard Beamis wasn't called "Big Dick" for nothing. He intended to steer the corporation to become the largest, the most profitable, in the New West. Hell, why stop there? Why not the whole world?

The main problem was, at the moment, Big Dick could not speak. Could not write. Could not make himself understood. He knew what he wanted to say but try as he might, he could not make the words come out. Earlier that week, when the speech therapist came to work with him, he grasped wildly for her hand, his eyes wide. He tried so hard to tell her, but the sound that came out of his throat meant nothing to her. He tried to write a message, but somewhere between his brain and his one working hand, the words got derailed. His message was a toddler's scribble.

"It's alright, Mr. Beamis. Richard. Big Dick. Can I call you that?" Her smile was genuine. If anyone could help him learn to speak again, this highly trained and sympathetic young therapist could. If she knew Beamis had undercut her employee compensation package, she gave no hint of it. "Learning to speak again takes time. We must be patient. With your good hand, point to what you want." She held a laminated chart with cartoonish drawings on it. A glass of water. A figure shivering. A figure sweating. A commode. Christ, he didn't need a goddamn drink of water, and he didn't need the shitter – somebody was trying to kill him, for fuck's sake! There was no picture of a masked man with a gun on the chart. He needed protection. He needed to get the hell out of here, out of his own hospital! Where was his wife? Where was his doctor? Where was his nurse? He shook his head no – at least, he thought he was shaking his head. He no longer seemed to be able to command his muscles to do their job. How to make this pretty young woman understand? Alas, the therapy session was over. She made an entry on the chart and left, leaving him alone with his suspicions.

Beamis was sure he had seen him, the tall figure in the black duster, Springfield rifle over his shoulder, like a rogue soldier. The shooter who had been killing old people, sick folks, had been picking them off one by one, but no one paid much attention. These were not mass shootings, these crimes received no press coverage, the headlines were all income taxes, immigrants, and influenza. And now he saw him again, outside his room, the Lone Gunman! Richard pawed wildly for the nurse call bell with his working arm but could not reach it. He roared out, bellowing like a beast, an effort that triggered his heart monitor to sound its electronic alarm, but still no one came to his aid. From inside his brain, walled off and besieged like the Alamo, he heard his wounded self whisper, *My kingdom for a nurse*.

The person who entered his room looked like a nurse, dressed in scrubs, carrying a standard issue Ruger 9mm in a sexy leather holster and wearing a Wellmart ID badge that said NURSETTE. He didn't recognize her. She must be new.

"I've got something for you, Mr. Beamis." In her hands, an empty syringe.

Boots Calhoun

At last, Boots Calhoun had a crack at running this damn rodeo. Already a card-carrying member of the High Plains Cattlemen's Association, she had her sights set on the Cowgirl's Fortune 500 Club. Although Calhoun was only Acting CEO, there was a good chance the title could become permanent if Big Dick Beamis didn't fully recover. While the cerebral vascular accident – the stroke – hadn't killed the old cigar- smoking coot, it had caused massive damage, leaving Wellmart's CEO pretty much useless. As long as he was holed up in ICU, Boots was able to get in and make some deals of her own; she held the reins of the biggest medicine show in the West. But as sanctioned CEO, her control could be even bigger. Dammit, she knew how to turn a profit. The key was in the Patient Satisfaction Survey. The PiSS reports were golden. Customer satisfaction was what really mattered. Customer satisfaction meant a resort-like atmosphere. Folks wanted a vacation. They wanted Wi-Fi, flat screens, plush mattresses, saunas, a driving range, shooting range, ammo sold at the gift shop. And they wanted the administrators to have well-appointed offices, covered parking, and electric charging stations for their luxury cars. Boots knew right where to find the needed funds. As Chief Financial Officer, she knew just where to make the deep cuts that Big Dick had been too soft-hearted to make.

It started with staffing, across the board cuts, chop- chop. The grippe made it easier, what with furloughs in place to prevent the bug's spread. She had already slashed unit secretary positions and environmental service personnel by half, furloughed medical records personnel, with no intention of bringing them back. Now, for the professionals. She began by replacing the nurses with unlicensed workers. Pretty waitresses – excuse me, servers – with big white teeth and ivory handled pistols slung from their hips, nursettes who knew how to push pills with a smile, now that's what the customers wanted. Nursettes who knew how to handle a gun, could goddamn shoot straight. Sell every patient a damn wrist monitor to record their vitals. Doctors could start their own IVs, push their own intravenous medications, change their own postop dressings. And family members could sit with patients at night, they could play cards at the bedside. That's all the night nurses did anyway, she had heard from a reliable source. Nursettes and housekeepers would be hired part time and work for tips, tin badges and WE ARE HEALTHCARE HEROES tee shirts. That would inspire them to go the extra mile with a smile. Cheap labor and customer satisfaction were key to profits, continued corporate growth. The customer was always right. Give 'em what they want and charge 'em for it. And those who didn't have benefits? Fuck 'em. Let 'em work for companies big enough, profitable enough to provide health insurance. Will it sink small business? Well, duh! Mom and pop can't afford to pay healthcare for their employees, but we sure as hell can't have taxpayers foot the bill. Oh, hell no. Bigger business means better business. Wellmart Corporation is the biggest cock on the block, and Boots Calhoun held that big, fat cock in her capable hands.

Bully Ratzer

The sheriff of High Plains walked out of Wellmart like a champ, having licked the grippe, having kicked it in the balls. In truth, he had been scared when it hit, robbing him of his breath, leaving him gasping. In truth, he was still a little weak, and his fat, ruddy face beaded up with sweat under his ten-gallon hat, in the heat of high noon. But now that he knew he wasn't going to die, he could safely say the bug had been nothing more than a bad cold.

Going to the hospital to seek treatment had been a stroke of luck, for Ratzer had accidentally discovered the whereabouts of that damned nurse, the one who had humiliated him with the enema, the one who had protected the porn sisters and who was still working to bring him down. Nurse Kit Carson was hiding out in Wellmart. Now that he knew who and where she was, the bitch was as good as dead. He would take no chances that she might recover and try to ruin his career again.

Before he could get into the vehicle, the reporters swarmed like mad cows, surrounding him, firing questions. He gave the cameras the victory sign and a winning grin.

"Sheriff Ratzer, can you give us a statement about your health?"

"Sheriff, are you still in the running for governor?"

"Sheriff, what are your plans to take down the grippe?"

"I have to say, I've never felt better. If that was the dreaded Chinaman's virus that ambushed me, I have to say I kicked its ass."

"Sheriff Ratzer, is the hospital still experiencing a shortage of protective equipment? Are the nurses and doctors properly armed?"

"Is there a cure for this damned bug yet?"

"What can you tell us about the care you received? Is it true there's a shortage of nurses and technicians?"

"There ain't no shortages, not in these parts. Wellmart is the best spa in the West. I just checked in for a little tune-up, that's all. The doctors have pronounced me fit as a fiddle, healthy as a horse, right as the rain."

Deputy Jones used his bulk to force an opening in the herd of reporters surrounding the luxury vehicle, opening the door. Ratzer plopped heavily into the back seat. The deputy closed the door and bid the driver to vamoose.

"Home, *Jefe*?" the driver asked.

"Not just yet. I need to make a little detour to Chinatown."

The driver glanced at his boss in the rearview mirror. Their eyes met. Understood.

High Plains' Hop Alley had sprung up down in the bottom land, near the railroad tracks, back in the 1870's. A past governor, Ed McCook, had actually invited the Chinese to the territory, back when California was trying to get rid of the bastards. Back then, that land was good for nothing, and the immigrants made use of it. Built their laundries, their grub joints, pot houses, and opium dens, lived in the backrooms. But the land was worth a fortune these days and the handwriting was on the wall for little family-run businesses. Ratzer knew his days of squeezing the Chinese were coming to an end, so he would squeeze 'em all a little harder today. One by one, he stopped at their places of business. They all knew what he was there for.

"Mister Sheriff, good to see you," Sing Li said with false deference. His Oriental Saloon, Pool Hall, and Restaurant was the most ambitious of Chinatown's establishments. "What can I do for you?" Unlike his neighbors, Mr. Sing would make Ratzer ask outright.

"I'll have the usual."

"You mean, Peking Duck?"

"I mean the cash." The sheriff sat at the nearest table, waiting for the protection money to be brought to him in a to-go bag. A mélange of smells, of oil and spices and garlic wafted from the kitchen. Ratzer realized he was hungry. Actually, Ratzer would have hated to shut the Oriental down. This was his favorite restaurant in town. Mr. Sing's Peking Duck was to die for, made fresh daily from fowl raised in the city's parks, caught after dark, and served up with a variety of savory side dishes, a gastronomic wonder. And while you were waiting for the food to be prepared, there was the massage parlor next door. That little China doll had such skillful hands. But not today. That grippe, that damned germ whose ass he kicked, had left him feeling tired, nonetheless. He was afraid his main man muscle might not rear its ugly head. Had that nurse managed to sabotage him? Had she slipped him a mickey? Switched out his blue pill for some other little blue pill?

Mr. Sing brought him a bag of hundos, on top of which was a white take-out carton of his famous dish. “Thank you, Mister Sheriff, for your protection.”

Ratzer nodded his accord and took his leave. From the back alley, the sound of gunfire. Ratzer pretended not to hear. It might have been a gentlemen’s duel; it might have been drunk cowboys. Maybe even Chinese fireworks. In any case, he had people to take care of that. Couldn’t risk any confrontations himself. As sheriff, he had friends in high places, but he had enemies in low places. He worked hard for the kickbacks, the bribes, the skimming. But he didn’t want to be a law enforcer forever. For him, the office was a steppingstone to the Big House on Fourteenth Avenue. Bully Ratzer wasn’t just any old body wearing a star. To ensure his reputation stayed clean, Ratzer had called on a rogue gunman to finish off Nurse Kit Carson.

Things were heating up, for a Tuesday night. The smell of burning incense, of opium, of joss paper – hell money – for the ancestors. Everywhere in Chinatown, red paper lanterns and the pop- pop- pop of firecrackers in the alleys. This was the night of the hungry ghost festival, or some such voodoo these superstitious Chinks celebrated. On top of that, you had your drunk Micks and Spicks trying to fight them, each other, and every other damn body in sight. Hell, let ’em. Li had delivered a bag of silver and Bully Ratzer had beat the grippe. Now his belly was full. Life was good again.

Then, a text from his best deputy: *Local forecast - Balmy Wether back in town.*

What, that little half- breed bitch was back? Now what in hell did she want? No good could come of that, not with the election coming up. He would have her picked up and driven out to the eastern badlands. Or at least as far as East Colfax. In any case, he needed to leave before the shooting got out of hand.

Balmy

They walked together, through the camps, toward Chinatown. High Plains did not hold good memories for her. She had lived and worked at the O.K. Corral Gentlemen's Club for as long as she could remember. Which wasn't really that far back. Something bad must've happened to her to cause her early memory repression. She had heard somewhere that the subconscious remembers everything – every image, every word, every feeling. But she remembered enough bad shit to bring down Bully Ratzer.

A bottle rocket whistled, a flash of light, over the rooftops of the carryout liquor stores, car rentals, immigrant grocery stores. A billboard – WELLMART'S HEALTHCARE HEROES SAVE LIVES – a bold banner above a team of masked employees wearing red, white, and blue spangled capes, their arms crossed like badasses. An orange- haired woman riding a wheelchair crossed the street, coming toward them, yelling, "Hey, kids, any utes got a smoke?" At least that sounded like what she said. But they were not Utes and no, they did not. They did not smoke. The woman cursed them and rolled away. The three walked on, falling in step.

The sound of gunfire, or maybe it was backfire, somebody's muffler. A Mercedes wagon slowed, like it was following them. Black, with tinted windows, impossible to see through. Was she being paranoid? Those luxury sport utility vehicles were common in High Plains. Or was it Ratzer's posse? The directions on her phone showed they were nearly at the rendezvous point with the reporter. Had they been tracking her through her phone all along?

Pancho Villa

Oscar Ramirez (a.k.a. Pancho Villa, the avatar on his I.D. badge) was Wellmart's Employee of the Month. His reward was to have his photograph on the wall in the hall of fame leading to the parking garage. He also got to wear a badge; a gold star made of aluminum. Although he did not give a damn about the award, he wore the badge on the pocket of his scrubs. He wore it because it entitled him to one free meal every shift he worked, all month long. It also entitled him to use the complementary Employee of the Month parking spot. Pancho rode a bicycle to work. He chained it to the metal post holding the sign that said Employee of the Month. He had a vehicle, a Bronco, but he had gotten popped with a DUI a few months ago and the sheriff had taken his license. He had not even been behind the wheel, but asleep on his couch. An anonymous caller had turned him in. Ratzer had shown up at his apartment and made a deal. Your license for six months, and a hundo for "processing fees." When Pancho showed up at the Sheriff's office six months and one day later, the clerk had no record of the charge and no license to return. Pancho was still mounted on two wheels, instead of four. But he felt better than he had for a long time.

Pancho had survived the cost containment cuts the department had been forced to implement. He was reliable, thorough, and had a friendly manner. Like most employees of the month, he went the extra mile. What that meant in corporate terms was that he worked overtime without pay, did tasks outside his job description, when asked, and made other people look good. Employee of the Month was the ultimate attaboy given to make overworked people feel appreciated. But the parking spot and the free meal, that shit was real.

And then he was approached, he was invited, he was tapped by the doctor herself. Halliday wanted him to join the vigilantes for healthcare justice. Would he help smuggle a sick patient *out* of the hospital? Damn straight, he would. The only good thing he had to say about the hospital he worked for was that it was clean. You could practically eat off the floor. And if the nurses were messy, leaving used IV tubing hanging after patient discharge, dripping its last few drops onto his clean, practically sterile floor, if the trashcans sometimes contained hazardous waste, it was because there were not enough of them. They were responsible for too many patients, all of them too sick, too injured, to take care of themselves. That was why they were in the hospital, not for a holiday, a spa treatment. The administrators did not take care of the patients, draw their blood, did not start their IVs, did not deliver their chemotherapy, did not change their bloody dressings, or empty their urinals, their urine bags, their bedpans, nor did they change their sweaty sheets, monitor their vital signs, or give them their medications. The doctors did not do any of that either. It was the nurses who did that. And it was the people in his department – Environmental Services – who kept the place properly sanitized. A hospital is not a healing place if it is not clean, orderly, and safe.

As Pancho dressed and gunned up for work that day, he felt a sense of pride in his work, something he hadn't felt for a long while. He was a vigilante for healthcare justice, invited by Doc Halliday herself.

Doc Halliday

Before starting her shift at Wellmart Emergency, Doctor Ruth Halliday went upstairs to look in on Nurse Carson, who had a bad case of the grippe. Expecting to find her much improved and ready for discharge, Ruth was shocked to discover, almost by accident, Carson stuck in the linen supply closet at the end of the hall, forgotten, dehydrated, "HELP ME" scrawled on the pillowcase in what looked like her own blood. Talk about short-staffing – my God, this woman needed skilled, 'round the clock nursing care! If she was to have a chance in hell of surviving, she would have to be taken someplace where she could get the care she needed, and fast. Halliday was a doctor, but she had no jurisdiction up here, on the floors. She was an emergency medicine doc; her domain was downstairs in the fast lane.

Standing there helpless in the linen closet, Halladay texted Tonto, but the Indian was apparently still AWOL, on a vision quest. He was off the grid, might as well be dead himself. Hopefully, he'd check his messages soon. The vigilantes meant well but they were rogues, every damn one. Available when it suited them. She missed her military days. An order was an order. You couldn't pick and choose your assignment; you simply did what you were told.

"Kit?" The nurse opened her eyes when Halliday spoke her name. Responsive; that's a good sign. Stethoscope to ears, she listened to her lungs, which sounded like a 1953 washing machine. But she was young and had no underlying disease. What she needed was fluids, postural drainage, ambulation – in other words, good nursing care.

"Hang on, old girl. We're going to get you out of here."

Halliday left to find the charge nurse. There was none. Not a nurse to be found on the entire floor. In fact, there wasn't an employee to be seen. Halliday put in a call to the hospitalist, Doc Adams, and headed for the elevators. She would go to the top and speak with Boots Calhoun, the acting CEO. Only a miracle could save Kit Carson now. The elevator doors opened; out stepped three armed guards.

"Doctor Halliday," the biggest one said. "We're here to escort you off the property.

"What is this, a joke? I work here."

"Not anymore, you don't. Come with us, Halliday."

Their faces impassive, their tin stars gleaming, the guards ushered her down the hallway. She couldn't very well resist; she was outnumbered and outgunned.

"I need to use the restroom."

"Make it quick. And don't give us any trouble." He touched the handle of the handgun in plain view on his hip.

Inside the stall, Ruth pulled out her phone and put in the call. The new recruit from Environmental Services was their last ace. Halladay hoped he could carry out the plan alone.

"Is this Pancho Villa?"

"At your service, Doctor Halliday."

"I've got a favor to ask."

Wyatt

The reporter was sitting at the back of the saloon, hunched over a plate of Chinese dumplings. Wyatt thought he recognized her from the news channel Abuela watched every evening. Polly Pry, that was her name. Big dark eyebrows and fake, plump lips.

"That's her," Balmy said with a little tremor of excitement. "That's Polly Pry. You boys wait for me outside, OK?"

"But –"

He felt a rip of pain, watching her walk toward the back of the saloon. She thought he was just a kid, and he longed to prove her wrong. To show her how capable he was. How understanding of whatever it was she needed to tell the reporter. And the truth was, he was hungry. The food smelled good.

"Come on," said Mike, nudging him in the side. "Let's go watch billiards."

Reluctantly he followed Mike toward the smack of pool balls from the adjoining room. Looking over his shoulder, he saw Balmy pull up a stool and sit across the table from the reporter. The way she straddled it, like she was riding a horse. Their heads were together, already connecting, deep in conversation.

Some serious pool shooting back at the tables. Men who knew what they were doing. Wasn't much drinking going on, not back here in the billiard room. That's how you can tell it's serious, Mike said. Serious players don't drink much. They watched a while, then got restless. More fun to play than to watch.

"Hey, Chica, I didn't know you worked here." Mike, following a young waitress back into the kitchen. Mike seemed to know a lot of people, way more than he did. Wyatt followed Mike who cajoled the waitress, hinting for a handout, an eggroll maybe, or a fortune cookie. But just then Mr. Sing appeared and scolded them. "Get on home, young fellas."

"We're looking for Zhang," Wyatt said, thinking fast.

"He's got work to do. No time for loitering."

Wyatt envied Zhang his employment. He wished he had a paying job. Then he would have some money to play pool, he'd have money to wager. Money to buy something to eat.

The two boys went back into the saloon just in time to see Balmy walking toward the exit, in between two figures, one male and one female. It looked like she was being escorted out. But the female was not the reporter. The reporter was nowhere to be seen. Wyatt darted toward them.

"Hey, Mister!" Wyatt called out loudly, to be heard above the bar noise. He didn't dare call out Balmy's name. The man, who had hold of Balmy's elbow with his right hand, turned to look at him, and as he did, he revealed the pistol in his left hand, aimed at her ribcage. Now shit started happening real fast, so fast that Wyatt didn't stop to think but pulled out his own pistol, puny in comparison to the guy's nine-millimeter, but Wyatt's hand was fast. At that very moment, the gun was part of his hand, like his joystick. He and the antique Smith & Wesson seven shooter were one. The room became a video screen, his gaze was wide, he saw everything. He saw and he reacted, squeezing the trigger, seeing the surprise on the man's face as he fell, feeling the kick against his palm, the sting, saw his hand jerk. Joysticks don't jerk. This was real. Balmy lurched, but the bitch cop coldcocked her with the butt of her gun, then turned it on Wyatt, but he was already firing. And again, he watched the bitch cop go down, her piece firing as it hit the saloon floor. Now the other customers were drawing their weapons and scrambling for cover wherever they could. Another shot rang out – it was not from his piece – and another, from the far side of the room. The sound of breaking glass, a woman's scream, and Merle Haggard singing "I think I'll just stay here and drink."

Suddenly, there was Mike, pulling Balmy away, pulling her by the legs across the saloon floor. Wyatt squeezed the trigger again, and the gun blew up in his hand. But his target was hit, the other cop was down. The saloon erupted in a brawl, the sound of cursing, glass breaking, everyone was fighting, it was a real barroom blitz. Someone grabbed his arm, it was Zhang.

"Come with me!"

Wyatt followed him to the billiard room where Mike had dragged Balmy under a pool table. Her eyes had opened, she was coming to consciousness.

"I've got a place you can hide," Zhang said. Supporting a dazed Balmy between them, they followed him to a liquor storage room where he locked them inside. "I'll come get you when it's safe."

"Dude!" said Mike to Wyatt.

"What?"

"Your hand. Are you OK?"

Wyatt still gripped the antique pistol, or what was left of it. But his hand was black with third degree burns, and parts of the gun appeared to be melted. Later, it would hurt like a sumbitch but right now he felt nothing but elation. They had saved Balmy from Ratzer's men.

Kit Carson

Doctors all but disappear when there is no longer a viable cure. They may write the orders for a compassionate extubation, or for compassionate amounts of morphine or hydromorphone, but those fuckers seldom stick around for the person's passing. So that explains why there were no doctors, but there were no nurses either. Maybe I am already dead? If so, purgatory was a linen closet, because that's where I seem to be, crammed between two stainless steel carts of blankets, sheets, and pillowcases.

No, wait, I can't be dead. I have kids to raise, lives to save, and a man's heart to win. This is no country for old nurses. *Don't give up yet, Kit. Gather your strength. Sleep and dream.* Dreams, like short, surreal film clips, unfolding on the screen behind my eyes.

The rumble, the song of his motorcycle – blocks away. I see him in the saddle, hair the color of steel, the hard curve of a bare arm. He stops for me and I climb on behind, though I cannot, for the life of me, remember his name. I cling to him as the machine flies, my face buried in his neck, his hair tickling my lips, my hands on his hips. I don't know where we're going but we're moving, I don't care where. I've never been happier than now. In this multisensory dream movie, the air is filled with green smells, just-cut hay, cottonwood seeds. Layers of coolness, layers of smells. Jump cut to motorcycle resting on its kickstand, he and I scrambling up an embankment to lie in the grass and pine needles. Wilson's Peak in the distance, endless blue above. He devours me. I can see his single tattoo, feel the scar on the skin covering his left flank, his latissimus dorsi. I trace it with my fingers, memorizing his back with my hands. Breathing in his sighs. Breathing out my own. The breeze whispers in the aspen leaves. This, this is Valhalla, this is The Big Valley in the sky. Below, I see my tombstone:

Here lies Kit Carson, Mother and Nurse,
She lived and she died
To pad the Corporation's purse

But wait, that's not how I want to die. No, it's all wrong. Stop the film, the video, whatever is playing. Press Pause, something's wrong. It can't end like this. But I can't press the pause button, I can't press the call button, there is no call button, and I can't seem to move at all. I'm back inside my head, I feel my heart pounding, I'm gasping for air. Outside my door, a tall figure, backlit, a silhouette. I'm afraid it is Death, come for me.

Pancho Villa

Standing at the foot of her bed, the nurse looked as lifeless as a dry leaf. He turned off the monitor alarms, disconnected the IV – it looked like it ran dry days ago – then scooped her body into his arms as if she were his dead bride, or maybe his child. Then, aware of someone standing just outside the door, he placed her warm body onto the cart – a covered cadaver carrier, the special gurney used to transport dead bodies, unseen, through hospital corridors. He pulled over the cover, placed a sheet and pillow on the top for the ruse. Out of the linen closet, looking past the stranger carrying a rifle, standing outside the door, down the long corridor to the service elevator. Press B for basement. Down here, the low hum, the slow heartbeat of the hospital, could be heard, it could be felt, an electrical vibration, rolling past the electrical room – RESTRICTED – the Engineering room – KEEP OUT – through the delivery door and into the waiting mortuary van where a team of first responders – vigilante paramedics and EMTs – worked hard to rehydrate and oxygenate Kit. The driver, a champion bull rider, drove like the wind to the old fort on the edge of High Plains where Tonto had set up a field hospital. From here, she would be transported under cover to her own home where she would either recover to fight another day or pass on to the next world.

In any case, Pancho's work here was done. For today. But now that he had a taste of vigilante healthcare, he was ready for more.

Lone Gunman

Willie walked down the corridor, his spurs ringing with each step. The rooms were occupied but the hallway was empty. He paused before the door at the end of the hallway, the closet where his victim was being housed, and watched as the orderly pushed the cadaver cart out. The gunman touched the brim of his hat in respect. He knew a cadaver cart when he saw one. Sure enough, the nurse's bed was empty. An IV infusion pump, standing at attention, but turned off. The plastic tubing, just removed, looped like a lariat on the floor. The name on the plastic bag of antibiotics confirmed it: Carson, Kit. Looks like Death's angel had beat him to it. He heard the ping of the elevator, the swoosh of the doors opening. There goes the body, off to the morgue.

Now that he was here, might as well earn his money. See if some other poor sonofabitch needed to be put out of their misery. From the supply cart he took a protective paper gown, hat, gloves, and mask. He covered his cowboy boots with blue paper slippers. Then, carefully wrapping another blue isolation gown around his thirty-aught-six, he rode the elevator up to the Intensive Care Unit to do a little side job. But someone had beat him to it. Richard Beamis was dead, his alarms ringing like a Wyoming wind chime, the tracing of his heart's electrical activity a line as flat as Kansas. From his bedside, a nursette looked up, a large syringe in hand, equipped with an 18-gauge needle.

"Help you?"

"I'm looking for Richard Beamis."

"Sorry, sir, he just drew his last breath."

Well, hell's bells, imagine that. Was the Grim Reaper furloughing him? Or maybe just limiting his practice to outside the hospital's walls.

Boots Calhoun

From her penthouse office, behind the heirloom mahogany desk that had belonged to Big Dick Beamis's robber baron grandfather, Wellmart's new CEO spoke to the reporter on the phone, in an official statement. The founder and former CEO had died of complications following a cerebral vascular accident – a stroke. She ended the call, quite pleased with herself. Actually, a bolus of air injected into his bloodstream by a nursette was what had killed him, but it is quite common for stroke victims to encounter second strokes in the first days and weeks following the initial ischemic attack. There was no reason to suspect anything else, no autopsy would be performed. His widow would get his pension and a sizeable life insurance payout, but she was not part of the company structure, she was not on the board of directors. Even if she questioned her husband's death and requested an autopsy, in High Plains the coroner was the sheriff. Calhoun then wrote out a sizable check to Bully Ratzer's gubernatorial campaign from Friends of American Healthcare, LLC.

Despite the breaking news implicating Sheriff Bully Ratzer in a sex trafficking scheme, no arrests were made. Ratzer continued to dominate in the polls. The people of High Plains didn't give the accusation much thought. Right now, the grippe was the hot topic. The story of Ratzer kicking the grippe's ass had more coverage than allegations about his supposed involvement in the sexual exploitation and prostitution of minors. This was, after all, the Wild West.

In Beamis's memory, Boots Calhoun poured herself a shot of his good whiskey and picked a Cubano from his private humidor, now that she held the keys. She licked that cigar, clipped it, and with a lighter from her own purse, lit it, gently sucking, her surgically tightened cheeks puffing, puffing, puffing. She knew what the hell she was doing. Kicking back in Beamis's ergonomic office chair, she put her bespoke snakeskin cowboy boots on the desktop and enjoyed a quiet moment of celebration.

Kit Carson

The crisp, smoky scent of burning sage. Wake up! Familiar voices, like birds chirping. Open my eyes to see their faces, a wreath around me, my family gathered around the deathbed, my deathbed. Not a hospital bed, but my very own queen size, PosturePerfect mattress, covered by my own saddle blanket. There's no place like home to die. Surrounded by my loved ones, attended by the best and sexiest nurse ever. I am still breathing, my heart is beating, and I realize I am hungry. He helps me sit up, and Grandmother brings me chicken soup. He holds the spoon, I sip the broth. Green chili bites my tongue, opens my nostrils. I am alive, I want to live.

*

We held the funeral that Tuesday, a small gathering of family and friends in the living room. The rosewood box on a pedestal, a wreath of tumbleweeds and prairie sage, a ribbon that proclaimed BELOVED MOTHER. Next to it, a photograph of Kit Carson in her prime, dressed in blue scrubs, edited with a pair of angel wings coming out of her back. Abuela, uncles, Mike – the Trujillos all dressed in their best, and my son Wyatt, cowboy hat in hand, a hand wrapped in white gauze from a burn, I was told. (Later, he would confess the whole truth, how he shot the deputy, then the next round misfired, burning his hand.) Beside him, Calamity, dressed in a white linen frock, her hair braided by Abuela's experienced hands and wrapped around her head like a renaissance crown. In her clenched fist, a bouquet of my favorite yellow wildflowers. Tough little weeds, dandelions. So restorative, their bitter young leaves.

A phalanx of healthcare vigilantes, stethoscopes looped like lariats around their necks, stood at attention in front of the woodstove. With ceremonial precision, Doc Halliday and Pancho Villa folded the white silk banner, upon which was printed HEALTHCARE HERO, which Doc herself presented to Wyatt, with a solemn salute. Tears welled in my eyes and slid down my cheeks. Tonto got up to speak, after which he passed the hat for The Caring Ranch, a nonprofit co-op hospital managed by nurses. Our mission statement: Let none who enter pay more than they can afford. Halliday advised me to choose a new alias, as Kit Carson was dead. That would take some thought. At that moment I was content to be nameless, newly born.

That night, by the light of the midsummer full moon, we made a campfire out back and buried the rosewood box beneath the cottonwood tree. On top of the mound of freshly dug earth, Calamity planted a popsicle stick cross on which she had printed R.I.P. HAMMIE. We sang Happy Trails to You and Tim, who had ditched the moniker Tonto, recited an Arapaho story about animal spirits, opened a bottle of whiskey to celebrate, and passed it around. Later, Zhang delivered Mr. Sing's Peking Duck, sixteen side dishes, and complementary fortune cookies all packaged in white take-out boxes. At midnight, Abuela served her pan de Muertos (bread of the dead) fresh out of the oven, to everyone's delight. As intended, the Mexican funeral food replenished my spirit as well as my body.

Later, when the guests had gone and the family was asleep, Tim and I sat outside under the stars, watching the logs turn red. He brought out his pipe and we smoked a bowl of a native weed believed to have curative properties.

"Kiss me, Kemosabe."

Our lips pressed together, we inhaled each other's breath, and somewhere deep within I felt the dry kindling of my libido reignite. Tim knew just what to do. He blew gently on the sparks, and before long we had a hot campfire blazing, a fire that lasted until dawn. Old night shift nurses like us, we are used to caring for others while the rest of the world sleeps. That Tuesday night, it was our own lives we were saving.

ABOUT THE AUTHOR

Linda Collison worked unarmed as a registered nurse in Denver hospitals for over a decade. *Nurse Kit* Carson's *Knife & Gun Club* was originally written as a series of five short stories published over a period of eight years. Available as individual episodes in collectible paperbacks, electronic, and audio format.

author photo - PhotoZ by Sheila. Sheila Zappanti

More fiction by Linda Collison:
Star-Crossed
The Patricia MacPherson Nautical Adventures
Blue Moon Luck
Looking for Redfeather
Water Ghosts
Holiday on Planet Jolieterre; a Nova Skylar Space Nurse Adventure

www.fictionhouseltd.com

www.lindacollison.com

www.ingramcontent.com/pod-product-compliance
Lightning Source LLC
Chambersburg PA
CBHW021736190726
48288CB00009B/3071

* 9 7 8 1 7 3 2 2 2 9 0 8 2 *